2 BETWEEN BAYS AND THE Sea

The Log of the Sherry D

A Sailing Adventure

Around the Delmarva Peninsula

HOWARD WALKER SCHINDLER

Illustrations by Diane R. Schindler

Copyright © 1999 by Tiller Publishing

ISBN 1-888671-29-7

All rights reserved under International and Pan-American Copyright Conventions. No part of this publication may be reproduced in any form or by any means — graphic, electronic, or mechanical, including photocopying, recording, taping, or information storage and retrieval systems — without the prior permission in writing of the publisher. The publisher takes no responsibility for the use of any of the materials or methods described herein, nor for the products thereof.

Illustrations by Diane R. Schindler.
Photographs by Howard Walker Schindler unless otherwise noted.

Graphic design and production by:
Words & Pictures, Inc., 27 South River Road South, Edgewater, Maryland 21037.

Printed in the USA by:
Data Reproductions, 4545 Glenmeade Lane, Auburn Hills, MI 48326.

Questions regarding the content of this book should be addressed to:
TILLER Publishing
P.O. Box 447
St. Michaels, Maryland 21663
410-745-3750 • Fax: 410-745-9743
www.tillerbooks.com

I dedicate this book to my wife and loyal supporter,

SHERRY DONOVAN SCHINDLER

the person for whom I named my boat, the *Sherry D*.

Also,

I further dedicate this book posthumously to

VAN OTHO WILKERSON

[July 20, 1952 - March 18, 1991]

one of the "Good Ole Boys" I describe in Chapter 12, later to become a true friend, companion and loyal supporter in this writing. He will be missed.

ACKNOWLEDGEMENTS

Jonathan Tourtellot — Senior Staff writer for *National Geographic* magazine, who was a member and friend on the Earthwatch Oceanographic Expedition to Palau, February and March of 1987. Jonathan encouraged me to write this book and advised me in much of the content of the manuscript.

Robert de Gast — who was the first person to make this passage under sail and, of course, it was his experiences that inspired me to follow his route. Robert helped me with his advice, comments and his encouragement. Without him, I would probably not have accomplished this voyage in the same premise as I did.

Doug Brown — Sportswriter for the *Baltimore Sun* papers, friend and neighbor. Doug helped me with the editing of the manuscript and advised me in reference to its content and organization.

Norine Fox — Retired A. A. County School Librarian of the Lake Shore Elementary School, and author. Norine not only encouraged me in my writing, but offered her expertise in editing, content and arrangement. She is a good friend and did a lot of the research and investigative work for me in the verification of my experiences.

There are many, many more who I would or should acknowledge, but you will find their names within the pages of this book, as actual names are used with their permission. There are others too numerous to mention here or persons who offered support or assistance but their names are unknown or they do not wish to be mentioned. There were so many people that I met on this voyage that either helped or in some way added to the contents of the story. These were the real ones who made the voyage interesting for me. Even in those very few cases of non-assistance, they, in their own way, added to the interest of this story.

Needless to say, this voyage would not have been at all possible without the stability, construction and sailing ability of my little boat — my pride, the *Sherry D*, a 1963 Sailmaster 22.

Table of Contents

Preface 8
Chapter 1   In Preparation 11
Chapter 2   Sea Trials 15
Chapter 3   Day 1 - Getting Started 17
Chapter 4   Day 2 - Across the Chester 22
Chapter 5   Day 3 - Tolchester 27
Chapter 6   Day 4 - Tolchester to the C&D Canal 31
Chapter 7   Day 5 & 6 - Chesapeake City, C&D Canal
                to Smyrna River & Bowers Beach 36
Chapter 8   Day 7 - Bowers Beach to Lewes, DE 47
Chapter 9   Day 8 - Lewes to Indian River Inlet 50
Chapter 10   Day 9 - Indian River Inlet to Ocean City Inlet 53
Chapter 11   Day 10 - Ocean City to Chincoteague, VA 59
Chapter 12   Day 11 - Chincoteague to Folley Creek and "The Good Ole Boys" 63
Chapter 13   Day 12, 13 & 14 - Cedar Island to Wachapreague 72
Chapter 14   Day 15 & 16 - Wachapreague to Oyster 78
Chapter 15   Day 17 & 18 - Oyster to Cape Charles and Pungoteague Creek 85
Chapter 16   Day 19 & 20 - Pungoteague Creek to
                 Pocomoke River and Beverly Manor 90
Chapter 17   Day 21 - Pocomoke River to Crisfield, MD 100
Chapter 18   Day 22 - Crisfield to Wenona 104
Chapter 19   Day 23 - Wenona to Bloodsworth Island 109
Chapter 20   Day 24 - Bloodsworth Island to Solomons Island 119
Chapter 21   Day 25 - Mill Creek to Knapps Narrows 125
Chapter 22   Day 26 - Knapps Narrows to Magothy River and Home 128
Epilogue 131
Reading List 135
Index 136

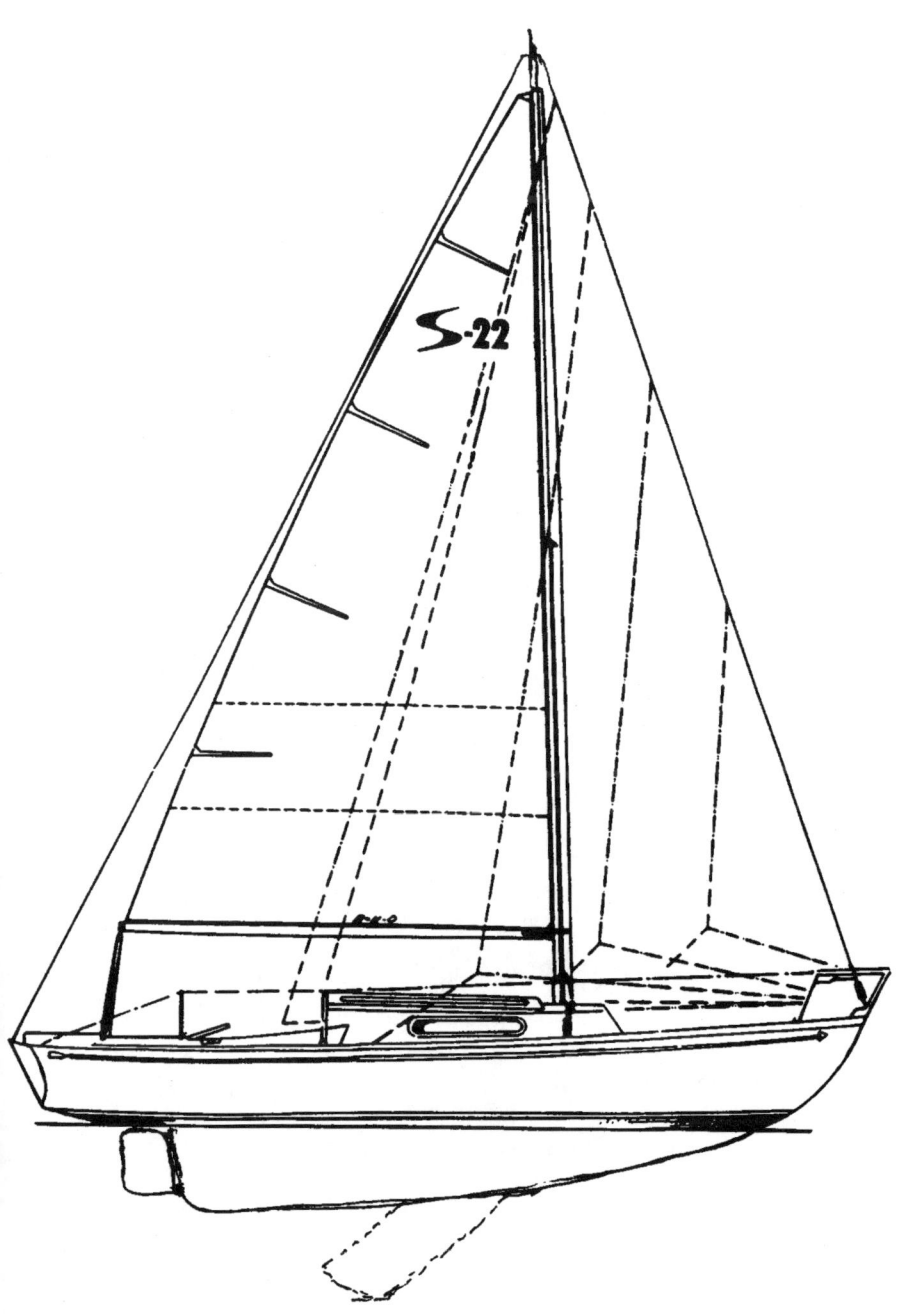

Sherry D - a Sailmaster 22

PREFACE

On the first of April 1987, I returned from an oceanographic expedition to the Island of Palau, one of the major islands of the Micronesia chain in the western Pacific Ocean. There, we had put a diver on the bottom of a toxic lake in our search for the origin of insular phosphate of the geologic past. This entailed a climb over a treacherous, mountainous jungle pass, backpacking loads of equipment, supplies and diving gear. We set up our camp, entered the lake and swam amongst millions of jellyfish in the crocodile-infested waters. We took our samples, conducted our studies, and survived. I returned home thinking I had done it all. Nothing in my future could ever surpass the thrill, the achievement and the satisfaction of that adventure. I was wrong! I came back home from half-way around the world and a month later embarked on an adventure that far exceeded any of my wildest expectations.

Years prior to this expedition, in the fall of 1977, a well known free-lance photographer and writer, Robert de Gast, spoke at one of our meetings of the Magothy River Sailing Association. Mr. de Gast had a passionate interest in ships, the sea and especially the Chesapeake Bay. He had previously written *The Oysterman of the Chesapeake* and *The Lighthouses of the Chesapeake*. That night, he spoke to us about his latest book, *Western Wind Eastern Shore*.

I agree with John Barth when he said in the Foreword to *Western Wind Eastern Shore*, that, "In May 1974, Robert de Gast did a simple, delightful and interesting thing that no one seemed to have thought of doing before. Mostly alone, mostly under sail, he circumnavigated the Delmarva Peninsula. *Western Wind Eastern Shore* is a narrative of de Gast's 24-day voyage in his sloop *Slick Ca'm*. This little vessel was a 22-foot Sailmaster, built in Holland in 1963. It was one of the first of the fiberglass hulls, and carried him not only around the eastern shores of Delaware, Maryland and Virginia, but behind its barrier islands and into its rivers, creeks and marshlands."

Slick Ca'm was the identical style of boat that my wife, Sherry, and I purchased a year before de Gast's lecture. We selected our boat, as did de Gast, because it was affordable, had a swing mast that could be lowered easily and a shallow draft that could get us into many of the coves and creeks that other sailboats could not. Yet, it was heavily constructed with a centerboard for stability and accommodations for overnight cruising. It was also a pretty little boat with nice lines. After the lecture, my wife bought me a copy of *Western Wind Eastern Shore* and gave it to me as an anniversary present in February 1978. By then it was apparent; Robert de Gast's lecture and his interesting book, plus the relationship of these two boats, had readily activated my appetite. I knew that someday I must follow the de Gast route.

As of this writing, I know of no other attempt to do this as de Gast and I have done. Thirteen years after Robert de Gast's circumnavigation, I planned my departure of the same for the 12th day of May 1987. I note here that many years have passed (twelve to be exact) since I made this voyage and now publish this book.

Many who had read the original log of the *Sherry D* and then the manuscript of the voyage encouraged me to publish it. They argued that many active sailors and even armchair sailing enthusiasts could learn from and enjoy reading this adventure. It would also be an inspiration to anyone who thinks that there is no adventure after the age of sixty. Maybe some will try and I encourage them to do so.

Many changes have taken place on our waterways since 1987. New waterfront developments continue to grow, spurred by increased population. Over-crabbing, over-fishing and pollution are still problems, although the past few years have shown reason to hope things are getting better. Boats have become even faster and more livable. Navigation has become easier and more precise, *i.e.*, GPS, depth finders, wind indicators, knot meters, and better radios with better weather stations. Cellular telephones plus many other advancements make sailing in the '90s a different experience.

Still, the challenge is there. The wind still blows, the sun still rises in the morning and sets at night. Tranquillity is still and always just around the next bend. What follows is my story.

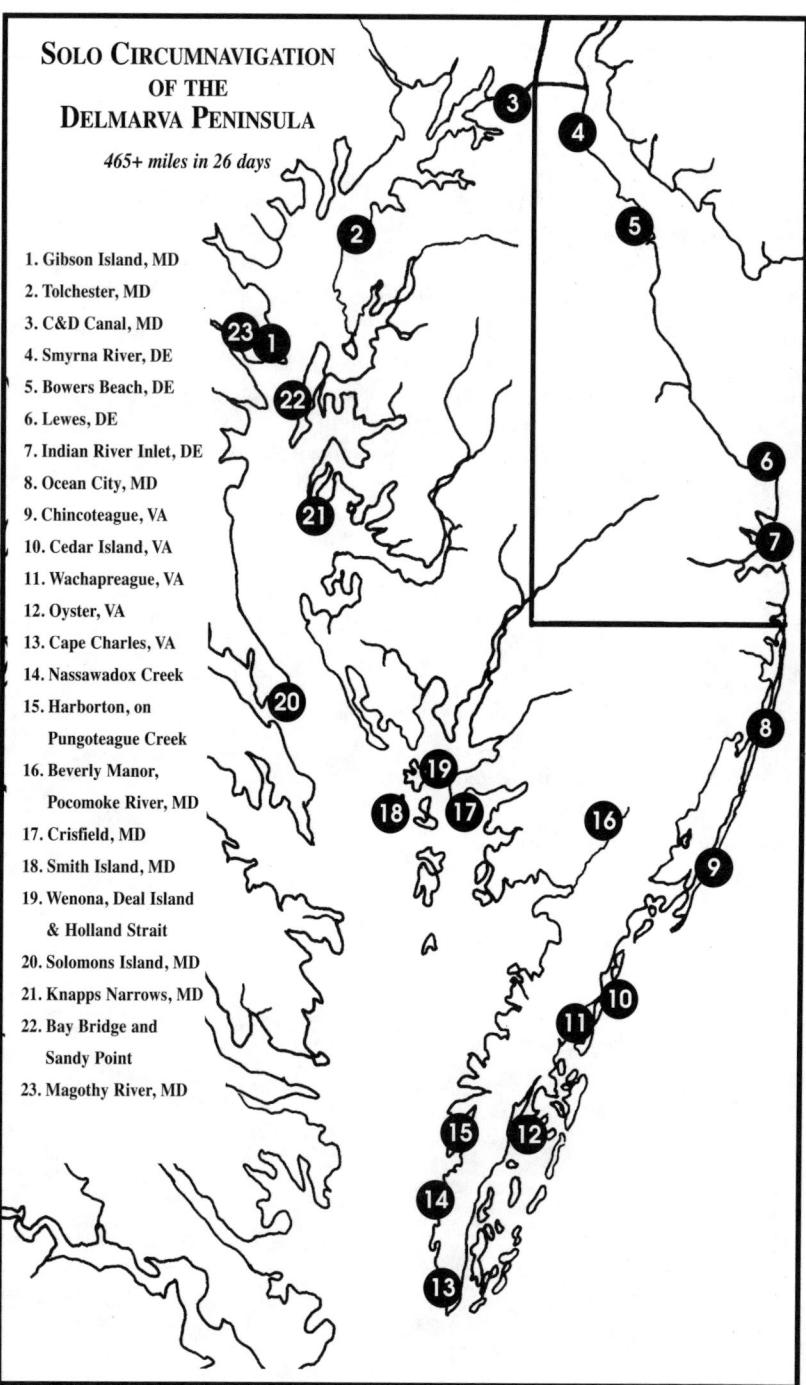

Chapter 1

In Preparation

The desire to make this voyage around the Delmarva Peninsula in my little Sailmaster, the *Sherry D*, had been in my mind since Robert de Gast's lecture in the fall of 1977. I became more enticed after reading his book *Western Wind Eastern Shore*. I was very interested in ecology and especially in the environmental aspects of our rapidly deteriorating Chesapeake Bay. It was obvious to me that if we ever intended to save the Bay, we must first start with the waters that flow into it. I wanted to explore these rivers, creeks and marshes first hand. I had the boat that could do it and I had the experience, as I had an oceanographic background and had worked for some time taking water samples and studying the ecology of the upper reaches of the Bay. What better way was there to do this than to do it as de Gast had done. I had no intention of writing a book about this experience, but I had planned to document my activities in my Ship's Log and to make a record only for my own information. The thrill of the voyage was the icing on the cake. This narrative is taken from the Log of the *Sherry D*.

There were many conflicting circumstances that prevented me from leaving home for any length of time and I knew that a trip like this would take the best part of a month. Each year hundreds of people sail around the Delmarva (the peninsula that connects the eastern shores of Delaware, Maryland and Virginia), and they can do it in a short period of time, taking the ocean route. In fact, each year there is a sailboat race around the Delmarva, called the "Great Ocean Race." It starts and ends at Annapolis and most racers can sail the entire course in three to four days, sailing around the clock. In my case and in de Gast's case, it was different. To follow his route would take me behind the barrier islands along the ocean side, enabling me to explore many of the rivers, creeks and marshes of the Delaware and Chesapeake Bays. I calculated averaging 24 to 32 miles per day and then to take time to explore some of the interesting rivers and places within the reaches of the Delmarva. It would take the best part of a month to travel the 465-mile circumference around the peninsula. Unless it was absolutely necessary, I would not sail continuously around the clock. I would find some nice anchorage or dock somewhere for the night. The trip would be a navigational play on tides, winds and currents. I would sail alone, for several reasons. For one, the boat was too small for more than one large person plus all the provisions for such a long trip. The other reason was that it did not appear to be a difficult trip and to solo would be an adventure. I looked forward to the experience. Now it was time to get busy. I had to prepare myself and my boat.

I had previously arranged to haul the *Sherry D* for clean up, bottom check and paint, plus a hundred other things. I would take the *Sherry D* to Ferry Point Yacht Basin on Mill Creek off the Magothy River in Anne Arundel County, Maryland, only a few miles from my home. My little boat was in need of much tender loving care. In my rushed winter schedule, I had left my boat in the water with only a small protective cover over the cockpit. I had taken the mast off her at the end of the past season in hopes of doing a lot of preliminary work over the winter. I did nothing, because in the fall of 1986, after my affairs were arranged so that I might be away for awhile, I made my decision to take this trip.

Then, in November, I received an offer from Earthwatch to go on an oceanographic expedition to the Western Pacific. This was too good to pass up, yet I had looked forward to this circumnavigation of the Delmarva for the past 10 years. I was not going to quit now and made up my mind that I would do both. After all, I would only be in the Pacific one month. I would leave March 1st for Palau as our expedition would be divided into three stages or teams. I was to be on the last team and would be involved in the diving and in the taking of the core samples. I would certainly be back home by April 1st. Then I'd have a month or more to prepare the *Sherry D* and be on my way no later than May 12th.

Robert de Gast had warned that the starting time was very important as it was necessary to get through the marshes behind the barrier islands before the first week in June, or be eaten alive by the mosquitoes and green-head flies. This meant that I should depart as soon as possible and no later than the 12th of May. On April 1st, I returned from the Pacific on what I then thought was an unsurpassable adventure.

Now I had to regroup, acclimate to state-side activities, plus clean up unfinished business, go through a month's mail, write many letters, do the hundred and one household chores that had accumulated in my absence. Suddenly it was April 22nd and I really had to get started on the preparation of the *Sherry D* if I were to make this trip at all. A few weeks before, I had notified the yard that I would have the boat there on the 22nd about 9 am. It was 8 am in the morning when I put the little four-horsepower Evinrude motor in the motor well and pulled the cord. She went right off on the first pull. Pleasantly surprised, I proceeded those few miles around to the south side of the Magothy River. This was a good test for the little kicker and she ran well. It was a beautiful Wednesday morning, after a

Freddy, at the yard, had her out of the water, washed down, blocked in her cradle and ready for me to go to work by noon.

week of rain (which was the other excuse I had used to delay the bull work ahead of me in preparation). The trip only took half an hour.

It was my first chance to get back on the waters of the Magothy River. The new structures along the shoreline that had sprung up over the winter amazed me. The Magothy was quickly being consumed by modern suburbia, like most of the other beautiful waterways of the Chesapeake. I couldn't help but think of my childhood on the river and how I used to sail my daysailer or paddle my canoe over this same route. It had been 13 years since de Gast had made his voyage. In these fast moving times many changes had taken place on our waterways. Time *is* change and I was sure that this solitude would not be here much longer. I wanted to study the bays, sample the waters, see the change and enjoy the tranquility before it was gone.

I was right on schedule and Freddy at the yard was most accommodating. He had the *Sherry D* out of the water, washed down, blocked in her cradle and ready for me to go to work on her by noon. The bottom didn't look bad at all, but I had to put a new thru-hull fitting in the drain from the galley sink where the old one had corroded away. I also had to rearrange the plumbing for the head and holding tank. I was able to continue work and had the little boat almost ready to paint by the next day. I scheduled her to go back in the water by Friday afternoon. Then the rains came again. It was Sunday afternoon before I could get a coat of paint on the bottom. With the bottom painted, two coats of polish on the topsides, a new thru-hull fitting in place and a lot of sanding done on the toe rails, Freddy raised her in the sling and I dropped the centerboard to paint and check the cable.

She was looking like a new boat now and we had her back in the water by mid-afternoon on Monday April 27th. I departed Ferry Point by motor, as the mast was still not installed — it lay on my bulkhead at home. There was a good 12-knot breeze right on the beam, and we moved well under the power of the little four-horsepower motor and the new bottom paint. I was home in 20 minutes and tied the *Sherry D* in her berth ready for the rest of the preparations.

Before May 12th, I had to strip and varnish the mast, sand and varnish all of the bright work, paint the interior of the cabin, mount the new radio especially purchased for this trip, mount and orient the compass, put in a new bilge pump and two new batteries, check all the lighting, step and rig the mast, put the sails on and trim them, provision, etc., etc., etc. I wondered if I would ever make it. If the weather held, I would.

Prepared

Chapter 2

Sea Trials

I had planned to have the *Sherry D* ready for departure no later than May 12th and to have an easy run to Worton Creek, some 23 miles up the Bay and on the Eastern Shore, the first day. It was a tight schedule, but I was confident. I knew that I could do it.

It was now May 17, I was already five days behind schedule and embarrassed. Would I ever cast off? There was one setback after another; always something coming up to impede my preparations. Each job seemed to take a little longer than expected. On May 10th I had raised and stepped the mast after checking all the rigging and installing my new radio antenna. A few wiring problems on the running lights took more time. Before I could get the final coats of varnish on, it had rained again. It appeared that there was no need to hurry now or get excited, but I did. It was getting late in the season and I must admit I was considering whether I should even go. I had put too much into this preparation to turn back now. If I didn't go this year, would I ever?

So, now on this beautiful Sunday morning, I was ready to bend on the sails and adjust the rigging. After lunch, my wife Sherry and I, along with our granddaughter, Beth, sailed the *Sherry D* out the Magothy to check all systems and to do the fine-tuning under sail. Both of these crew members had been my staunch supporters. The wind was just right for fine-tuning and I went around loosening or tightening the stays and shrouds until I had just the right weather helm. The *Sherry D* performed like a professional and I was pleased. We headed back

Well, are you or aren't you?

just about the time the wind slackened. I lowered and furled the sails, then started the little motor. I noticed that the motor ran smoother with more power when I was on the foredeck. This was an indication that the more weight forward, the better. I couldn't adjust the height of the motor shaft in the motor well, but I could adjust the height of the stern from the water surface with ballast to allow more air to get to the motor from under the transom. I must remember that when loading.

It was a beautiful day, a nice sail in light air. Spring was in full bloom and it was 90 degrees. The boat was ready and my spirits were high again. All I had to do was to put my supplies on board in the morning. I had been accumulating things for a month and to put everything in its proper place and distribute the weight would be a job in itself. I saw nothing to hold me back now, and I planned to leave in the morning. All systems were go.

CHAPTER 3

Day One – Getting Started

Monday - May 18th, 1987

Yesterday had left me with such a good feeling. I couldn't sleep, knowing that I would finally be on my way, and yet I had so much to do. The longer I stayed awake and thought, the more I remembered all the things I had forgotten.

I was up early. My wife had to be off to her job. I would be gone before she returned home, and we made our last minute plans before she left. We had planned to meet in Wachapreague, Virginia, over the Memorial Day weekend, if not before. We planned to be in contact by radio/telephone throughout the trip. It was a beautiful morning and the weather forecast was "clear, sunny and hot with temperatures in the low 90s." The barometer was holding steady, but afternoon thunderstorms were predicted.

I drove my daughter, Diane, to work and said good-bye. On the way home, I stopped at the marine store to pick up some things I thought about last night — spare fuses and an extra inexpensive compass. I didn't trust my regular one and wanted a double check. Then I went to the printer to make extra copies of the hull and rigging diagrams, plus some technical information on the boat that was just nice to have along. Next stop was the grocery store for those last minute perishable items — milk, bread, eggs and a dozen other goodies that I could have done without. I thought about stamps to take along, just in case I wanted to write a letter and could find a mail box while ashore; so, off to the Post Office. I had thought about these things while laying awake last night and even considered that I would also place the stamps in zip-loc plastic bags, just as I had done with matches and anything

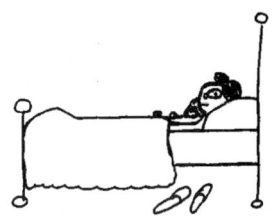

Just thinking.

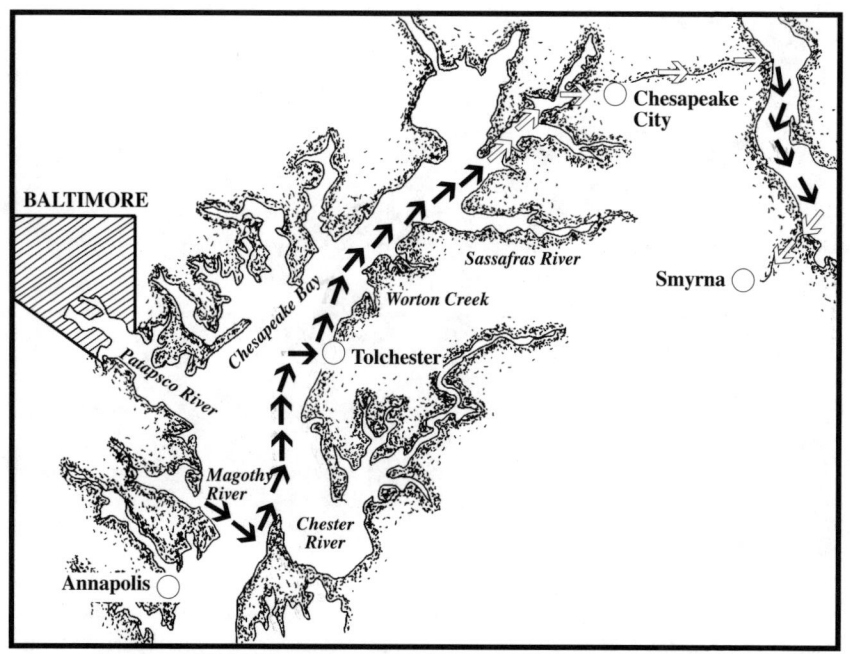

else that had to stay dry. Once back home, the phone was ringing and I made the mistake of answering it. More of my precious time was taken. When would I ever start loading this accumulation of gear? Once I was on the boat and underway, no one would be able to contact me. I was ready to take the phone off the hook and get to the business at hand. My itinerary indicated that I would sail from my home on the Magothy River to Worton Creek, some 25 miles the first day. Even now, there was no way that I would make Worton Creek today. It was already noon.

After lunch, I started the load plan. Previously, I had placed like things in like places. Now they all had to be carried from the house to the dock and then placed on board. There were dry goods, pre-made ice in milk cartons and frozen foods in the freezer, charts and navigational equipment, tools and extra line, clothing, first aid supplies, extra cans of gasoline, oils, kerosene for the stove and alcohol to light it with, etc. I had filled my water tank with fresh water the day before. I began to lose all semblance of my stowage plan. I was overloaded and everything was just thrown in.

While I was in the middle of this mess, I heard the Navy's Blue Angels fly over. This was Monday, May 18th, and they were performing their annual spectacular of aeronautics over the Naval Academy and the mouth of the Severn River in salute to the graduating class of 1987. I had always made a point to visit the Academy during this exercise because these guys were so great to see. This was the first time in 12 years that I missed their performance. As I looked at my overloaded boat, I wondered if these precision fliers were ever this disorganized before they climbed into their planes for their next adventure.

It was after mid-afternoon and I was finally ready. The sky was hazing over in the southwest, but there was no wind. It was *slick ca'm* (lower Eastern Shore talk for calm water), like the calm before the storm. I took off anyhow and motored around the Grachur Club point. The little boat moved right along even though she was loaded to the gunwales. This was really not how I wanted to depart, but in a few days I would be using up most of these supplies. I checked my new hand-held knot meter and found that I was doing four knots with the motor not nearly at full throttle. Not a ripple was on the water.

Less than a mile from home I was passing Henderson's Point. The wind came up on my stern and the haze turned black, chasing me right out of the Magothy. Was someone trying to tell me something? The wind gust caused little white and churning ripples across the water. This was where the Magothy becomes wider. The skies cleared

The load plan.

It was overloaded and everything was just thrown in.

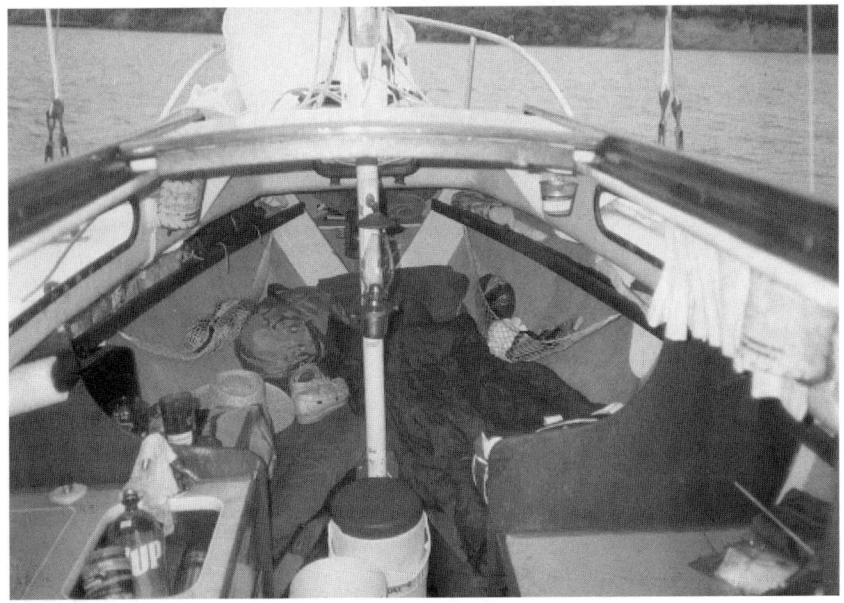

All systems are go.

but the wind continued strong. I was still under motor and it looked as if the storm was going to blow over. My new hand-held wind indicator recorded the wind at 10 knots out of the northeast. I had thought it would have been more. A Force 3, not bad! Now I thought it was all worth it. I raised the genoa (the large head sail or jib) as I had it already on, cut the engine and checked the knot meter. I was doing four knots with only the genoa. By 6:30 pm I had gone through the narrows at Gibson Island and headed for Baltimore Lighthouse. I couldn't ask for better conditions. I still had about two hours of daylight left and wanted to use it all. In the Bay, I could better check the apparent wind direction and either head across the Bay to Gratitude, which would be best, or, if need be, stay on the western side and spend the night in Bodkin Creek. I did want to get further along.

The weather forecast was not good for tomorrow. It called for rain, much colder (about 60 degrees — it was 90 degrees today). Winds would be 15 knots from the northeast. If I could get across the Bay and into Gratitude tonight, I would be in a much better position, wind wise, to sail north up the Bay tomorrow. I was sailing nicely now and holding a course on 90 degrees that would take me right across the Bay. I was finally on the first leg of my journey and in the Bay. It was a beautiful evening, my spirits were high, and I nibbled on an apple and ate a cupcake. South about four miles, was the Chesapeake Bay Bridge. It was a beautiful sight. The Blue Angels had flown today, and yesterday 50,000 people made the Annual Bridge Walk, an event sponsored by the Maryland Transportation Authority. People from all over the state and perhaps even other states come to walk the 4.03 miles across the William Preston Lane, Jr. Memorial

Bridge on this Bay Bridge Day and to be awarded a Certificate of Participation. I had done this myself in 1982. What great scenery, what great activities! Maryland has so much to offer and now I would be seeing so much of it. I had waited ten years since my original planning for this trip and this experience.

I raised the mainsail. The sails set fine, and I stood down in the cabin with my head above the hatch and steered the *Sherry D* by the steering lines. At that time the wind slackened, after a few minor shifts, and the Bay went like glass. I was about a quarter of a mile NNE of the Baltimore Lighthouse and had about an hour of daylight left. There was no choice, I dropped the sails, started the motor, and went back behind Gibson Island to anchor for the night. I made it there before dark and anchored where I could get an early start in the morning. This would be a good time to straighten out. I wasn't hungry, and couldn't get to the ice box or the stove for all the supplies laying about. The cabin was a mess and I had to do something about it.

I had traveled ten miles total since 5 pm and was only five miles into my trip. Only 460 more miles to go and already six days behind my schedule. At least this was a start and worth all the preparation.

At last, open water.

CHAPTER 4

Day Two – Across the Chester

Tuesday - May 19th, 1987

Morning came early, but I did sleep well last night. I had started to put things in their place but grew tired fast. I was asleep as soon as I stretched across the bunk to place some items on a shelf above. It rained during the night, at one point so hard that it woke me. I got up and closed the hatch boards. The wind was blowing strong and it was getting colder. The anchor was holding well and I was glad to slip back into my sleeping bag.

By 6 am I was up, washed and dressed. A cold front was moving in from the NW and a chop was on the river. The wind was blowing pretty good and there was a slight drizzle. I was anxious to try out my one-burner kerosene stove. I had tested it on shore and it worked well there. The stove was an important part of my equipment as there are no restaurants around the corner out here! For safety reasons, I tried to light the stove in the cockpit rather than inside the tight little cabin. The burner on a kerosene stove is warmed first by burning alcohol in a small cup at the base of the burner. When the alcohol is about to be expended, the burner should be hot enough to vaporize the kerosene, and it is just at that moment that you turn on the valve for the kerosene. If the burner isn't hot enough, sometimes the liquid kerosene will shoot up, ignite and burst into a large flame. Should this happen in a small boat such as mine, it could be dangerous. I was hungry, but I knew that if my boat went up in flames, I would quickly lose my appetite.

The stove wouldn't work outside in the open cockpit, and I figured that the burner was being cooled by the wind and the drizzle. When I cleared a space inside the cabin on the floor just below the open hatch way, the stove worked beautifully. There was still no room to work while cooking. I had to move everything off the top of the icebox to get to the cold stuff, then put it all back to get to something else. This was no way to bake a cake, but finally I did manage some bacon and eggs, along with a fresh pot of coffee. The weather was getting worse.

To wait it out a little longer made some sense. Again, this was my chance to organize. It didn't take long and the more I was able to put under bunks and into drawers, the faster I was able to move around. It is also extremely important to know exactly where everything is stowed. On a boat, in rough seas or at night in the dark, you shouldn't have to look for anything. You want to be able to put your hands right on whatever you might need. The important things should be in accessible places. This was my load plan. I felt good about it and sat down to have another cup of coffee. I decided also at this time that it might be a good idea to make and wrap a sandwich for lunch and brew another pot of coffee to put in my thermos. The way the wind was blowing, I might not have a chance to go below to fix anything later in the day.

About 10 am, a number of larger sailboats came out of Sillery Bay and passed me. There must have been 15 to 20 of them. Everyone was in foul-weather gear and they looked quite professional. I wondered if this was the day for the start of the Great Ocean Race. It would take them on much the same course as mine but would be non-stop. And, they would take the outside ocean route out of Delaware Bay and south down the Atlantic to Cape Charles, before coming north again, up the Bay.

I have a friend who sails this race every year. In fact, when Bud Jenkins had learned about my journey — as a joke, I hope — he presented me with a Bud Jenkins survival kit consisting of exotic canned goods, raisins, candy and granola bars, which I now had on board. I reached for my binoculars, but couldn't find Bud's boat. Later, I learned that these guys were not part of that race, but possibly some sailing club that had rafted up in Eagle Cove behind Gibson Island the night before, as many do.

The weather forecast was right, for a change. It was 60 degrees, a

On a boat, it is extremely important to know exactly where everything is stowed.

In rough seas, or at night in the dark, you shouldn't have to look for anything.

You want to be able to put your hands right on whatever you might need.

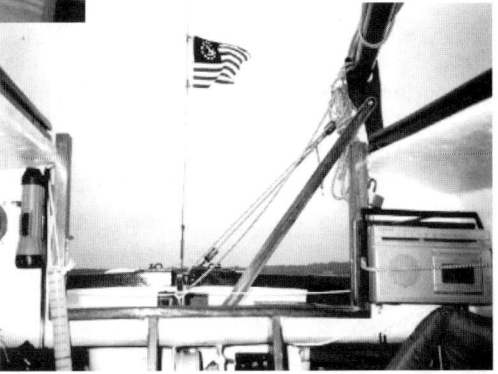

drop of 30 degrees from yesterday. The radio called for drizzle, but now it was raining. The winds were out of the ENE about 10 to 15 mph. Worton Creek was about 20 miles northeast up the Bay and all of the conditions were against me. Even the tide was ebbing, but it was getting close to a low. I thought to myself, "If I'm going on a trip like this, I can't have good weather all the time and if I'm going to make Worton Creek today, I have to leave now. Might just as well get my feet wet, go for it."

By the time I had everything in order, the working jib on in place of the big genoa and the anchor up, it was a little past noon. Out in the Bay it was blowing hard and there were 2 to 3-foot waves with white caps. Winds were right out of the NE and on my nose if I were to take a course to Worton Creek. The radio was now announcing small craft warnings on the Bay, but I was determined not to turn back. I wanted to see what the little boat could take as I might run into much worse than this later on. I had to change my course now and head SE across the Bay and in front of Cape St. Clair. Visibility was only about a mile, but I was on a course that would take me close to the Eastern Shore side of the Bay Bridge. I was sailing in the exact opposite direction to what I wanted, but had to in order to tack, come about again, in a position more favorable to the winds in order to sail north up the Bay. I was across the Bay in no time and came about to head on a northerly course which would take me across the mouth of the Chester River.

I checked my wind gauge and found 16 knots and gusting to 20+. I couldn't head up enough and, in fear of too much strain on this dear 25-year-old lady, I went forward in this pitching sea and took a reef in my roller main. Now I was sailing with the little jib and only half a main. I checked the speed and found I was doing five knots and holding a good course. Not bad for an old lady with shortened sails.

Across the wide mouth of the Chester, it was really blowing, 20 to 25 knots and gusting to 30+, with waves gaining in momentum and height. For the most part, they were 3 to 4-feet, but on occasion I would go down into a trough and couldn't see the shoreline. I could have sworn that there were six-foot waves at times. This is unusual for the Bay, but I had previously been in six-footers in the much wider southern Bay in larger boats.

There are some that might dispute my estimate that I bucked 4 to 6-foot seas while crossing the mouth of the Chester River. However, in August of 1933, Thomas Steinhise, the keeper of the Seven Foot Knoll Lighthouse that once marked the entrance to the Patapsco River and Baltimore Harbor, risked his life in a daring and successful attempt to save the lives of five seamen from the tug boat *Point Breeze* that sank off Seven Foot Knoll. During the rescue, Steinhise braved 15 to 20 foot seas with a temporarily stalled motor in his 24 foot dory. To commemorate his bravery, the Department of Commerce awarded Steinhise the Silver Lifesaving Medal on November 16, 1935. In March of 1989, the non-profit Lady Maryland Foundation moved Seven Foot Knoll Lighthouse to Baltimore's Inner Harbor, where it now rests in memory of Thomas Steinhise.

The Steinhise family members, along with volunteers from Wheelabrator Environmental Systems, and the city of Baltimore joined forces to restore the lighthouse that had deteriorated with the passage of time. The restorers have done a remarkable job and today, one may visit this memorable lighthouse which rests on the waterfront side of Pier 5. The Steinhise Exhibit is open to the pubic and is worth visiting.

I was the only fool out there with sails up. I had seen a few of the other big guys under power and a couple of the commercial fishing boats heading back into Rock Hall. The group of sailors that I had seen coming out of the Magothy had disappeared. They must have sailed south on a broad reach and were flying. My boat was handling beautifully. She sailed by herself and it seemed as though the harder the wind blew the better she sailed. I had just the right weather helm, with the center board lowered about half-way to give her the stability she needed. The boat headed just a little into the wind. I was wearing a safety harness that I tied to the mast, but now I went below to retrieve a life jacket and put it on over my foul-weather gear. It was getting colder and the spray coming over the bow was no help. I stood in the companionway to keep warm and let the *Sherry D* sail herself. The boat was great, but I didn't know if I could make it.

In terms of sailing, the mouth of the Chester River produced the highest seas that I experienced on the entire trip. Not necessarily the most terrifying, as there were more to come. I was now only about 12 miles from home and learning fast what my little boat could do. It was so rough that I thought of taking shelter in Gratitude on Swan Creek, or in Rock Hall; but the boat was right on course, the speed was terrific and I wanted to make up for lost time. I checked the charts even though I knew these waters well; Tolchester stood out as the next good shelter after Gratitude. If I couldn't make Worton Creek, I'd go into Tolchester. One thing in my favor was that I had an incoming tide and the currents were pushing me right up the Bay. The waves were over the bow and the rain had slowed to a light drizzle. The boat stayed fairly dry inside, which was a pleasant surprise. It was 2:45 pm when I passed Gratitude, on course and moving. It was getting colder, however. It looked as if Worton Creek would be a welcome sight.

It was about 4 pm when the wind began to blow back to the north and I had to tack. My little boat could do a lot of things, but the only thing she couldn't do was to sail directly into the wind. The best any sailboat can do is to sail approximately 45 degrees into the wind and, therefore, demand that the helmsman sail a zig-zag course to his destination, thus doubling and sometimes tripling the distance from A to B. I was right at the entrance of the Tolchester Channel, and the tide began to change. Now everything was against me and Worton Creek was still seven miles away. The wind was still strong but the waves diminished a bit after I passed the mouth of the Chester River. It was getting colder (down to about 50 degrees), and I was looking to put into Tolchester as soon as possible. Each time I made a tack, the wind would shift a little more. About 5:30 pm, I was ready to make my last pass into the Tolchester Marina. I hadn't seen a ship all day and now a large auto carrier out of Baltimore rounded buoy R"2" marking the channel north. I was about 500 yards offshore and west of the channel. The captain of that ship must have read *Western Wind Eastern Shore*, and thought he was to come up

Starboard!

on me just at this time. Robert de Gast ran into this exact situation when he was making his run to Worton Creek. Like Robert, I went below to get my camera. There was no way that I would cross the channel in front of that big bow and, of course, I veered off to avoid the bow wake. I took my photo even though it was drizzling and I was bouncing around. My picture didn't turn out well, but at least I got one for the record.

After the ship was clear, I came about and started my run again into the channel of the marina. At 6:30 pm, I was finally in the entrance and headed for the nice little cove where I had stayed once before a few years back in another boat. This was the first "slick ca'm" water I had seen all day. The cove was well protected, without a ripple on the water, but the wind whistled through the trees surrounding the cove and bent the trunks of the large pines. I felt safe inside and dropped anchor, lowered my sails and checked everything out. I took off my life jacket and foul-weather gear. I had to put some things that had been knocked around back in their place, but found the cabin dry except for a few places. Those I wiped up and dried as well as I could, especially my pillow.

I then lighted the stove, closed the hatch and warmed the cabin. For the first time this day, I sat back, relaxed and did nothing. "Happy Hour" came to mind and I fixed a strong Rusty Nail (Drambuie, Scotch and a very little water). I deserved it and felt good about the day's experiences. The growling in my stomach reminded me of a can of clam chowder I had stashed away. It was a good time to get it out while the little stove was going. My radio worked well and I transmitted a phone call right through all that bad weather, via the marine telephone operator. All was well at home and they were glad to know that I was okay.

The radio weather indicated much of the same tomorrow, but warmer. I stretched out, thought about the day's activities and how great the trip was. I learned that my little boat was everything I had hoped she would be. I felt secure with her. Had it not been for this weather, as bad as it was, I would never have known these things. I was glad it was behind me, however. Tomorrow I might pass up Worton Creek and head straight for the C&D Canal.

Tolchester. This was the first slick ca'm water I had seen all day.

CHAPTER 5

Day Three - Tolchester

Wednesday - May 20th, 1987

When I awoke, it was early and raining hard. I rolled over and went back to sleep. Later, I awoke to cold water dripping on my face. Oh no, water was coming in where it didn't come in yesterday. I couldn't understand. Why now? Yesterday, waves washed over the entire boat and I didn't have this problem. I wanted to sleep more, but that was out of the question. I had to do something before my bunk was soaked. It was time to wipe up and put some containers around to catch the water.

This I did and then stretched back on the other side of the bunk and turned on my portable AM/FM radio. With only one eye open, I fumbled with the radio dial. It just happened to hit on station 93 FM-Channel 13 TV. The news, weather and music came in clear as a bell. It was really a good station and I lay there for a while just listening. The station was so clear that it amazed me, and then I realized that this was a Baltimore station and in actuality it was only abut 20 to 25 miles due west of my location on the other side of the Bay. After that sail yesterday, it seemed as though I should have been half-way around the world.

The weather report was not good; we would have a repeat of yesterday's continuing showers, heavy at times with winds out of the north, 20 to 25 miles per hour. Gusts increasing in the afternoon. This would continue through the entire day and possibly through tomorrow. Some good music and cheerful talk came over the radio, which raised my spirits somewhat after that depressing weather news. I was comfortable and now closed the other eye only to have another cold drop drip on my forehead. This brought me back to reality and reluctantly I got up, washed, dressed and started breakfast. This time after eating, I put everything back in its place. The rain began to slack off a little. I studied the source of leaks and got out the caulking compound. The seals around the port lights and, most importantly, around the mast step where the electrical wires came into the cabin definitely needed some caulking. It was now 9:30 am and almost high tide; the tide would still continue to come in until 11 am The rain started again and the wind picked up from the northeast. The winds, tides, current and weather were all against me. I wanted to go, but my better judgment said to stay put. This I did and again took the opportunity to better organize.

The rain slackened and I decided to pull up anchor and move into the marina to purchase a few items and look around. I had been to Tolchester many times as a boy with church outings on the old Bay Liners. I remembered it as a wonderful old place with its big wooden and splintered pier jutting out into the channel. Up on the hill, a number of picnic tables had surrounded the covered pavilions built for just the kind of weather we were having now. For us kids, the best of all was the great amusement park with its tremendous roller coaster that seemed to ramble all over the hillside. What a great place for our church outings!

Now that has all been replaced by a modern marina. I tied up alongside the bulkhead and, once ashore, found a marine store fully stocked and a full-service marina capable of handling any type boat. I seemed to be the only non-working person around, and although the employees were busy doing their thing, they all had time to be pleasant and chat a little.

When they found that I had sailed that little boat across the mouth of the Chester River yesterday, the conversation got around to "which was the roughest body of water on the Bay?" Of course, each had his opinion, but it was pretty much agreed that the mouth of the Chester can get pretty trying in a northeaster. These guys became interested in my trip and gave me a lot of good tips. Most said that they liked being in that sheltered marina and didn't envy my going out in the bad weather, but they did envy me my trip.

Next to the marine store, I found some washers and dryers, and then a nice restroom with showers. It was even warm inside. I was invited to use any of the facilities and rushed back to the boat and pulled out everything that was wet. This filled both dryers. While my things were drying, I took a walk out to the jetty overlooking the Bay and looked to the north. If I had gone, the wind would have been right on my nose and it was blowing a gale. The currents and tide would have been against me.

As I walked back to the warm dryer room, I could hear the boats rocking in their slips with the waves pounding against the hulls and the halyards clanging against the aluminum masts. The rain had slacked to a light drizzle now, and I carried my nicely folded and dry things back to the *Sherry D.* I was tied to a good calm berth and no one was telling me to move. It was past lunch time and my stomach was reminding me of that. I ate my already prepared peanut butter and jelly sandwich and heated up the remaining coffee. It was a good time to just lie back, relax, and read a little to wait it out. A friend who knew that I was about to take this trip, and who was a jovial type Maryland history buff, recommended that I read John Barth's *The Sot-Weed Factor* prior to departing. I didn't have a chance to read the book before my departure, but did obtain a copy to take with me. This was a good time to start reading.

Sherry D docked at Tolchester Marina.

It was about mid-afternoon when I noticed a much larger sailboat come in and tie up a little farther down the bulkhead. Two fellows in foul-weather gear got off and went into the marina office. I learned that they had sailed up from Annapolis and were headed for the Sassafras River. They had had it, and asked the marina if they could leave their boat there. They could, of course, and they called their wives in Annapolis and asked to be picked up. At about 5 pm, the weather was looking better from where I sat in that nice sheltered harbor. The tide was slack now and should be coming in at any time. The radio weather indicated that things should clear up by tomorrow afternoon. It was only seven miles to Worton Creek, but the wind was still out of the northeast. If only I could get to Worton Creek, I could surely make it to the C&D Canal by tomorrow night. I decided to try and motor that 7 miles and, if all went well, I would be there by 7 pm. When I cast off, the large sailboat was still resting alongside the bulkhead and I assumed the two guys had the car heater on while on their way back to Annapolis.

The fact that the weather was looking better inside the marina was deceiving. I found out once I passed through the jettied channel and out into the Bay that the wind was blowing hard and I checked my wind speed indicator. It would jump between 20 and 25 and I was not doing too well motoring. The wind and the waves on my bow kept knocking me back. The favoring incoming tide running up the Bay was no competition against the wind that overpowered all other forces. I thought my little motor needed some help, so I donned my safety harness and life jacket before making my way to the foredeck. Once I raised the working jib and that head sail was set, my little boat pointed right up and began to pick up speed. Waves crashed over the bow as I inched back along the cabin to the cockpit, holding on for dear life while the *Sherry D* sailed her way into the wind. I was doing so well under sail that the motor was spinning in free water. I shut it off and raised the mainsail to the still fixed reef point. Now I was flying and heading up the channel just as I wanted, but the wind was still out of the northeast, and I found that I couldn't head up enough to stay on course. I tacked and took a new course towards Pooles Island, thinking that if I could make that, I could come about again, and if worse came to worst, head into Fairlee Creek, which I knew was also a good harbor.

I was about two miles from Pooles Island Light and about two miles from Tolchester when the wind increased to 25, gusting to 30 plus. I was getting drenched and I came about to see how well I could point up now and to see if all of this was worth it. No way! I found that I was making very little ground and couldn't maintain a course in any direction I wanted to go. This was crazy. I wouldn't even make Fairlee Creek before dark. My better judgment took over again, and I turned to a broad reach and headed back toward Tolchester. The *Sherry D* took off like a horse heading for the barn. Now the self-steering was ineffective on a reach in this type of wind, and the waves knocked her all around as we went between crest and trough. It was like taking an evening sail in the North Atlantic in the middle of February. My little Sailmaster was having a ball. I could almost see her smile as she crashed down on each wave and spread white water. On the crest, her stern would wiggle and bubbles formed in her wake. The wind whistled in the rigging and the rudder hummed. After all, this was her kind of weather. She was built in the north of Holland just for this kind of water. I began to feel as if I also caught her spirit, but I wasn't sure how much I could take physically. It was like being on that old Tolchester roller coaster again.

Within 30 minutes, I was back in the safe harbor of Tolchester, wet, cold and tired. I thought of the nice shower room that I had seen earlier and again tied up alongside the bulkhead. No one was around but I found the shower room was unlocked just as if someone there knew that I would return. It didn't take long to dig out some dry clothes, my shaving kit and the other pair of boat shoes that I had dried in the dryer this afternoon. I had been out only three days, but to shave, brush my teeth and comb my hair while standing up straight and looking into a real mirror was a treat. The hot shower was great. I didn't want to get out.

Back on the boat, I was ready to anchor for the night so I retreated to my little cove. There was not a ripple on the water there but the wind cut over the land mass and whistled in the rigging. This was a great anchorage and I hung the anchor light in the rigging hoping it would stay lit in all that wind. The kerosene stove worked like a charm and warmed the cabin. Canned spaghetti and meatballs tonight. I was somewhat disappointed in losing another day, but elated over the exhilarating experience. I felt I deserved a reward and mixed another Rusty Nail while the spaghetti was cooking.

Now time for the bunk. Tomorrow is another day. Even though this weather is expected to continue, I may just luck out.

An evening sail in the North Atlantic.

CHAPTER 6

Day Four - Tolchester to the C&D Canal

Thursday - May 21th, 1987

The rain beat hard on the cabin top during the night, but I slept well. Apparently, I had managed to seal a few of the leaks, most importantly the one over my head. I still had a few leaks that were not bad but annoying. It was 6:45 am when the sun beamed in through the port lights. I jumped up thinking I had overslept. I pulled the hatch cover back and looked out only to see an overcast sky off to the west, but it was the clearest I had seen in three days. I wanted to leave in about an hour as the tide would be slack by then. It was low now and I should be able to pick up the flooding tide to carry me north.

I turned on the radio weather and found that I could expect a 30 percent chance of showers and turning colder. The wind was out of the northeast, less than 10 miles per hour. I was again discouraged but determined to go. By the time I had a light breakfast, packed a sandwich for lunch, cleaned up and tied everything in its place, it was past 9 am. There seemed so much to do and every time I turned around, there was something else. I remembered that I had to fill the gas tank from the extra six-gallon tank that I had lashed to the foredeck. This meant having to untie the lines holding the tank and carry it aft where I could siphon the gas into the three-gallon tank that was attached to the motor in the lazarette. There must be a better way, but on such a small boat, where weight was important and I had to carry so much, this was the best I could think of.

The wind seemed to be slacking off, however, the tree tops surrounding my nice little anchorage were still being knocked around. The weather was clearing but continuing with a little drizzle. I started out well prepared, put on my foul-weather gear, had the safety harness and a life jacket in the cockpit. Everything

Two beautiful Labrador retrievers ran out along the bulkhead to wish me a safe journey.

was buttoned up for some more heavy sailing weather. I had raised the sails while still at anchor, shook the reef out of the main but left the little working jib on. Under sail and with the motor running, I proceeded out of the Tolchester jettied entrance. Two beautiful Labrador retrievers ran out on the bulkhead and sat there as I made the turn into the channel, as if they were wishing me a safe journey. As I passed, they followed me along the bulkhead. I couldn't resist and turned around, got my camera and took a picture. That seemed to satisfy them and they turned back to the marina. At the next turn in the sheltered entrance there was a group of mallards. Again photos were taken — another five minute delay. Oh well, that's what this trip is all about.

As soon as I was in the Bay, I was able to head northeast and paralleled the Eastern Shore. With motor, and sails close hauled, I was doing five knots. If I could remove the little working jib and raise the genoa, I could turn off the motor and keep my present speed. I had both head sails already on the foredeck and ready to go if I could keep them from getting tangled with each other. I had pre-arranged the lines so that I could tie one sail or the other on deck. Changing headsails in rough weather by yourself is a real trick and if anything gets tangled in a bucking sea, then you are in trouble. You could be knocked overboard or a sail could rip. Anything could happen.

Everything went like clockwork. The working jib was down, the halyard changed to the genoa and the big headsail raised, unfolding nicely as it came out from under the little jib. I tied everything down and went aft to cut off the motor, stowing it in the lazarette. I trimmed the sails and took off like a "bat out of hell." Things were now going my way for the first time. I sat in the hatchway steering with the steering lines and went right up the ships' channel. All of a sudden there it was, another large ship bearing down on me. I thought of my wife, Sherry and the time we were in this same predicament in the *Sandpiper* (our 35' Davis Yawl).

The engine was not working and there was no wind. Should I run a frying pan up the mast so the ship would see us on radar? It was a frightening near-miss that my wife never seems to let me forget. This time, I just sailed out of the channel. The wind slacked and I was glad I had the genoa up.

As we passed Still Pond, the sun came out but the winds shifted. This meant that I had to tack now. I could see Howell Point at the mouth of the Sassafras River. It looked hazy to the north, but I took a chance and opened the forward porthole to allow air to blow through. I looked up and saw patches of blue sky — maybe we were past the worst of it.

The wind is now out of the northeast, my heading is northwest and I'm sailing close hauled on a starboard tack. The mouth of the Sassafras River is to my right. I see Betterton off in the distance and the black clouds are hanging there. The worst storms are always at Betterton, how well I know. I was in a bad one there in 1975.

It is now 1:10 pm. I'm pointing up nicely, and the Elk River is just ahead, I'm on my way to the C&D Canal. I can hear gunfire from Aberdeen Proving Grounds and can see Havre de Grace to the northwest and Turkey Point off my port bow. It's 2 pm and I'm already into the Elk River. The winds are favorable now, but I am still close hauled. I'm headed across the Elk River and White Crystal Beach is my sighting point. White Crystal Beach is appropriately named as it consists of hundreds of little houses, all painted white. It is beautiful, so out comes the camera. Directly behind me is a ketch from Sweden, under power. We wave to one another. I'm still in my safety harness and that probably explains their puzzled looks as they pass. After all, they are in a 48-foot boat, under power with four passengers aboard and it is clear now.

The *Sherry D* is still approaching the C&D Canal. It is lovely here with so much activity. What a trip — what a day! I have sailed a lot in the Southern Bay and now this is the Northern Bay. If I was asked which I liked the best, it would be hard to answer, as each has its own special characteristics and each is completely different. One is just as beautiful as the other, each presenting its own challenges. It is necessary to see both.

I thought I was acclimated to the sun but, by mid-afternoon, the sun was bright and I was fooled by the morning haze. I was really burning. By 4 pm, I was at the entrance to the C&D Canal. I pulled over to the side, dropped the anchor and took down the sails, as you must motor through the canal and there is a big sign at the entrance that says so. I needed gas, but had enough to get me to Chesapeake City. By 5:30, I was pulling into the Corps of Engineers' anchorage and gassed up at the Dockside Restaurant where a nice young fellow filled my tanks. Even though the gas pumps were closed, he was kind enough to unlock them for my six-gallon sale. I was beat, and asked if they would allow a "dirty ole sailor" in their nice restaurant. "Of course they would," he said. The Dockside turned out to be a private yacht club which anyone can join for a dollar. It was a great place, nice people. I learned much from them about the restoration of Chesapeake City. I also learned that this part of the Eastern Shore was horse

Chesapeake City Dockside Restaurant and Yacht Club.

The Army Corps of Engineers Anchorage Area.

country. Some of the largest race horse farms are not far from here and Windsfield was one of them. Northern Dancer, one of the most valuable breeding horses, was still there. The young fellow who opened the gas pumps for me was not only the manager of the Dockside Restaurant, but he worked at Windsfield and was also a horse trainer. Woodstock is another horse farm and this is where Kelso, another famous horse, is buried. One may take a tour of the farms and the Dockside manager offered to take me around if I would stay over. As much as I would have liked to do that, time was a real factor now and I had to take a rain check.

Sherry D *tied to the Dockside Yacht Club pier.*

I understand that Mrs. Richard Alair du Pont III and five other investors formed a group in 1985 to restore Chesapeake City. The idea was to buy properties from persons who wanted to sell and then restore those properties to their original structures. If a person did not want to sell, but would rather continue to live in their home, then the group would lend that person money, materials and even labor, at no interest, so that their homes could also be restored.

Mrs. du Pont acquired and restored the Bayards Inn, originally built in 1835, with a very nice inn, lounge and restaurant. There are nice bed and breakfasts, shops, and, of course, the historical buildings are open for inspection. The town is now thriving; and the people are happy and considerate in their welcoming of visitors. When I left, I was a member of the Dockside Yacht Club of South Chesapeake City. I walked around the town, saw these sights first-hand and was pleased. It was time to turn in, so I made my way to the *Sherry D*, motored out to the center of the Engineers' Harbor and anchored for the night. Tomorrow I'll go through the canal.

Above: Bayards Inn, originally built in 1835.

Left: The Old Pump House once controlled the locks of the original Chesapeake and Delaware Canal.

Chapter 7

Day Five – Chesapeake City, C&D Canal to Smyrna River

Friday - May 22nd, 1987

I woke up to a beautiful morning. Some boats had already left and two large power boats, with powerful engines, were moving out of the anchorage. I wanted to return to the Dockside and top off with fresh water for my tanks as I didn't know when or where I would find good water next. By 7:45 am I had eaten breakfast, cleaned up, dressed and motored over to get the water. It was beginning to haze over and looked as if it could start to rain at anytime. At 9 am, after topping off the water tanks, I decided to call my wife and tell her I was about to go through the C&D Canal.

Since it was necessary to motor through the canal, I cranked up the little four-horsepower engine and left the sails furled. I followed the course of the larger power boats out of the anchorage area, made a right turn out into the canal and motored east toward the Delaware Bay. It was still hazy, but not threatening. The little motor strained as the boat pushed against the current. I had miscalculated the tides, as I forgot that we were on Daylight Savings Time and it would be another hour before the tide would be in my favor.

To compensate, I sat on the cabin top just forward of the mast and steered by the steering lines. My weight pushed the bow down and raised the stern just enough to allow more air to come up under the motor well and feed oxygen to the carburetor. The motor smoothed out, but our over-the-bottom speed was about 2 to 3 knots per hour. The water passed beneath the hull giving the impression of a much greater speed. It was a nice ride, and I enjoyed just sitting there watching the sights as we passed through the canal, 14 miles without incident. Half-way through the tide changed, and now we were being pushed by the currents along with the force of the engine. It did make a difference.

I was hoping for good weather as I had heard how unpredictable the Delaware Bay could be. All of the sailors I had ever known seemed to dread the Delaware. Even Robert de Gast quotes from the *Cruising Guide to the Chesapeake*, "Yachtsmen may argue violently about the relative merits of the Chesapeake and the coast of Maine, they may differ eloquently about the cruising merits of Long Island Sound compared to Narragansett Bay. But, there is one body of water on which there is complete agreement. They all dislike it with varying degrees of eloquence according to their gifts of self-expression. They are speaking of course about the Delaware Bay." Robert de Gast further says, "The Delaware does not offer pleasant sailing, but some of its fringes are strikingly beautiful, particularly the area around the Smyrna River." I was heading there, and couldn't wait.

At 1:30 pm I enter Delaware Bay. The sun is out, but hazy in the distance. Winds are out of the SE and they're right on my nose again. I will try a course to G"1N" and then follow the ships' channel to R"6L" about 14 miles, then into the

Ships passing through the C&D Canal.

Smyrna River. My sighting will be a tower on Delaware Point. I am using full sails, as the wind is light. I'm only 35 minutes behind schedule — not bad! Let's see what the terrible Delaware will bring.

I spotted a large ship coming out of the C& D Canal. She must have been only a few miles behind me while coming through the canal. I was crossing the ships' channel, and I didn't know if she would head towards Philadelphia or come south to the Atlantic. Sure enough, she came south and started to bear down on me. I had lots of time and crossed the channel with plenty of room. She was picking up speed, however, and her bow wave pushed water all over me and the cockpit.

After being in the Delaware Bay almost an hour, I found her to be a peaceful lady. The ships' channel is right there and it is impossible to miss sighting Domes Island Nuclear Power Plant, just 5 miles due south.

I was going great, a favorable 5 to 6-knot breeze was taking me right down the ships' channel. The sun was bright but still hazy. I realized I was just passing the power plant which was spewing smoke that would make Vulcan gods jealous. It looked as if it covered the sky from Wilmington to Newark. I began to think that as beautiful as the Bay, rivers and canals are, up close there is litter and pollution everywhere. I remembered going through the canal, speed boats were chasing up and down, big power yachts throwing a wake that threw my boat from side to side, causing havoc down below. Some were considerate and would slow down for me in the Canal, but most would just fly by with their fishing gear bending in the breeze. They would come close enough to see this "lonely old kook" and wave without looking, as if that would satisfy their nautical commitment.

The wind is veering now and it has become very hazy — time to tack. We're doing well, the *Sherry D* and I; she is sailing like an old pro, we are a great team. She sails and I write. The Delaware Tower was still visible 180 degrees from R"6L" and I know I'm not far from the Smyrna River. The jetty at the entrance to the Smyrna is deceiving and I'm not sure whether to enter on the north or the south. My charts showed the jetty with five feet marked right in the center of it, and one foot on each side. I played it right and went in on the north. (That's two for two — I also played the tide in Delaware Bay right. I took the ebbing at the entrance to the Bay and backed off one-half to one hour, then Daylight Savings Time gave me an extra hour and carried me right down the Bay.)

What a sight to see. The Smyrna River was nothing like I expected. I was looking for a nice quiet river with coves and tree-lined banks like our Magothy River. Here there was nothing but marsh with a channel running through it. I was under sail with the motor in the lazarette and looking for shelter to lower the sails. But instead, the wind was blowing across the marsh, the tide was coming into the river and we were running with it. The river twisted like a snake through the marsh. I was spellbound. Sometimes I was close hauled and heeling, next I would be wing and wing (the mainsail on one side, the jib on the other to catch wind from behind.). Occasionally a large crane, or egret or some other beautiful marsh bird would flutter from the edge of the marsh and fly on ahead of me, only to meet at the next turn. As I sailed along I was snapping pictures left and right. I thought the bridge where Robert de Gast had stopped, and where I now planned to stop, would always be just around the next turn. I would have the bridge in my sight as I looked over the marsh grasses, only to lose it again around the next turn in the river. We kept going and going in pursuit of that elusive span. What a thrill!

My thoughts were interrupted by a loud engine noise. I thought it was a swamp boat such as you would find in the Florida Everglades. I wondered what we would do if we approached each other at one of these bends, as the river was too narrow to pass comfortably. But, to my surprise, a small bi-plane came swooping just over the swamp grasses. Apparently, he could see me as my sails were much higher than the grass, of course, and he was looking down. Just about the time he was about to take my mast off, he must have pulled back on the joy stick, as the old plane angled up like a car on a racer's dip.

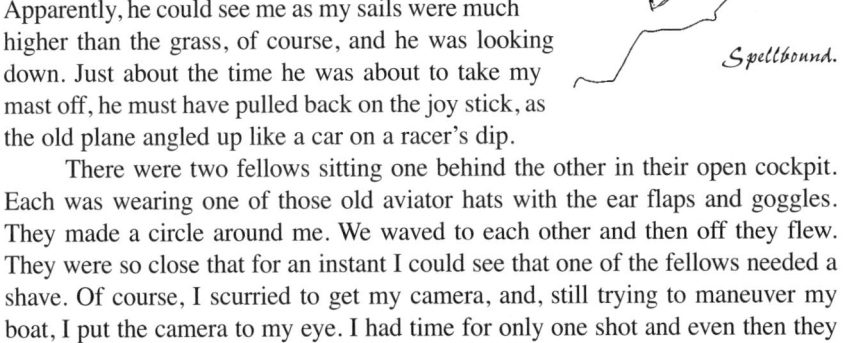

Spellbound.

There were two fellows sitting one behind the other in their open cockpit. Each was wearing one of those old aviator hats with the ear flaps and goggles. They made a circle around me. We waved to each other and then off they flew. They were so close that for an instant I could see that one of the fellows needed a shave. Of course, I scurried to get my camera, and, still trying to maneuver my boat, I put the camera to my eye. I had time for only one shot and even then they were too far away.

About then, we were rounding one of the bends and the wind hit me dead in the water. The channel was very narrow, and I knew I couldn't tack and I had no idea what the depth was so I just kept on going. I had my center board about one-third down and used it as a depth finder. We were now going in all directions with sails flopping and lines tangling. It was time for the motor. I had never put the motor in that quickly. I didn't even clamp it down. She went right off on the first pull. The motor was all I needed. Along with the current, I was able to maintain steerage. The wind was blowing hard and we were speeding down the channel. Finally, I rounded a bend and there was the bridge. I still had the sails up, made a turn with the motor running and came into the wind to drop the sails on the foredeck (now I was heading back out the river). I noticed the water gushing past me, but I was going backwards. It was crazy. I wondered if I had overslept and was dreaming. For the first time, I realized just how strong the current was. Once I had the sails down, I began to make headway. All of a sudden the boat turned — the current had grabbed her. I was on the foredeck. She took off full force heading directly for the mud bank. I just held on to the forestay and let her go. She ran right into the reeds and the soft mud with the motor still pushing her in. After we hit, I ran to the stern of the boat and turned off the motor. We were not moving any longer as the bow was stuck there in the soft mud.

The first thing to do was get organized. I furled the sails and flaked the lines, stowing everything in its proper place. Then I grabbed my big oar and pushed us out into the current. Immediately I restarted the engine to prevent the current from carrying us into the bridge. Once again I had control and we motored over to a dock which was in dire need of repair. It looked like an old fishing dock with crab pots and traps all around. There was, however, a brand new eight-foot-high chain link fence surrounding the area, but the area was deserted. I tied up to a piling, making sure the *Sherry D* was completely secured. It was an interesting old place and a good one to get ashore, stretch my legs and look around. The bridge and the road were but a stone's throw away. As I started toward the bridge from the dock and through the yard, I realized that I could not get out of the yard. The gate was locked and the fence was too high to climb over, from the inside or out. What a dilemma!

I decided to reboard the *Sherry D* and, while still tied to the dock, I could take a long line and try to drift back with the current to the bridge. Once alongside I could climb up on the bridge and thus onto the road. What a great idea but a little foolhardy. I kept having to tie lines together to get enough length. The current played havoc, and I almost went overboard. The bridge was blocked off to traffic, however I felt like a real celebrity. Cars kept coming to the bridge, pausing long enough for the drivers to look and turn around. No one said anything, and I thought that the two guys in the plane had put the word out in Smyrna that Robert de Gast had returned.

Finally, help arrived. Two men in a car stopped at the bridge to do some fishing, and asked if I needed help. They suggested I throw them a line, but with the current at about two knots, we had a terrible time trying to tie off. After much struggling, we were finally successful, but I was still not where I wanted to be. There was no place to climb off onto the bridge and go to shore, as the current prevented me from pulling myself close enough to the bridge platform. I knew that in the morning I would have to get on shore to untie the lines. My biggest concern was that if the bow line broke, we would go crashing into the bridge.

One of the men seemed to know the water and was telling me about the tides and currents. The tide would be coming in for five hours and going out for seven hours. I calculated that I had started in at 4:30 pm with an incoming tide. There would be slack, and then the outgoing tide would start at 9:30 pm. At slack, I could adjust the lines by myself. I did just that, and at 10 pm the outgoing tide started and the *Sherry D* was being whipped all around. This kept up for seven hours. I did manage to disembark during the slack and walked up to the road and found a barrier across the bridge, and the reason why all the autos had turned around. The cars were still coming and people mistook me for the bridge tender. I was asked all sorts of questions. Mainly, why was the bridge closed? How do you get back to Rt. 13? How far is it to . . . etc., etc., etc.?

Finally, reality struck and I realized all these cars were not coming to see me but were, in fact, heading to the beaches for the start of Memorial Day weekend and using this bridge as a detour to avoid the traffic jams on the major roads and bridges. But, to their dismay, the bridge was closed! The bridge was in terrible shape and could not have withstood the weight of all those cars. It was in such bad shape that I was concerned that the *Sherry D*, tied to her pilings, could pull the bridge down with the strength of the current. No wonder the bridge was so dilapidated. This was the Fleming's Landing Swing Bridge, and it appeared that a hand had not touched it in maintenance since the day it was built in 1913.

The mosquitoes had arrived and none of my protective sprays seemed to be helping. They were really bad. Once back on board, I sprayed the entire boat with "Black Flag" and decided to make up screens to protect me during the night, but I had nothing but bad luck in this endeavor, as the *Sherry D* was bouncing around too much, bucking the outgoing tide. Finally, I broke out a bottle of Avon's "Skin So Soft" lotion that I remembered having on board and applied some to my bare spots. Someone told me that, if I was going into the marshes, not to go without it. Sure enough, that helped ward off the mosquitoes. At this point, however, I was so tired, I just threw my sleeping bag over my head and fell into a deep sleep.

At 4:30 am I awoke with a start. The *Sherry D* was sitting calm in the water. I went up on deck and discovered there was a slack, and the incoming tide was just starting to pick up momentum. I thought of the strain on the bow line and worried about her slamming into the bridge should that line part. Surely my trip would end right there. Just as an added precaution, I threw an anchor out as far forward as I could and then let out about 10 feet of extra line and tied it off to the mast. I felt a little more secure now and headed back to my bunk.

Sherry D tied off to Fleming's Landing Swing Bridge.

Day 6
Smyrna River to Bowers Beach

Saturday - May 23rd, 1987

At 7:30 am, I awoke to a beautiful morning. The boat was riding well on the incoming current. The tide was up pretty high and I had about 2½ hours to go, before it would start running out. The information I was given last night was right on the money. The bridge, of course, was still blocked off to traffic. The weather forecast called for clear and sunny, with temperatures in the 80's today but a 40 percent chance of thunderstorms predicted for the afternoon. I should be heading into Lewes just about that time. I got cleaned up and had breakfast. I wanted to be ready to go as soon as the tide started changing. This should be an interesting day!

At 10:45 am the tide was still slack, and I climbed up on the bridge to take a photo, then back on the boat I reloaded my camera in anticipation of what might lie ahead on my journey today. I was ready to untie. I motored out; no sails this time, I was taking no chances. With a two-knot current and my four-horse-power motor, we moved out. I sat on the foredeck and steered with the lines, camera in hand.

As I came out to the Bay, Old Domes Island Nuclear Plant (by now I was calling it "Dooms Island") was visible to the north. Two huge Air Force cargo airplanes, a big C-141 followed by a C-5, were making their approach into Dover Air Force Base just 15 miles inland. After spending a night in the wilderness, this all brought me back to the reality of the world in which we live.

As I came out to the Bay, Domes Island Nuclear Plant was to the north. By now I was calling it "Dooms Island."

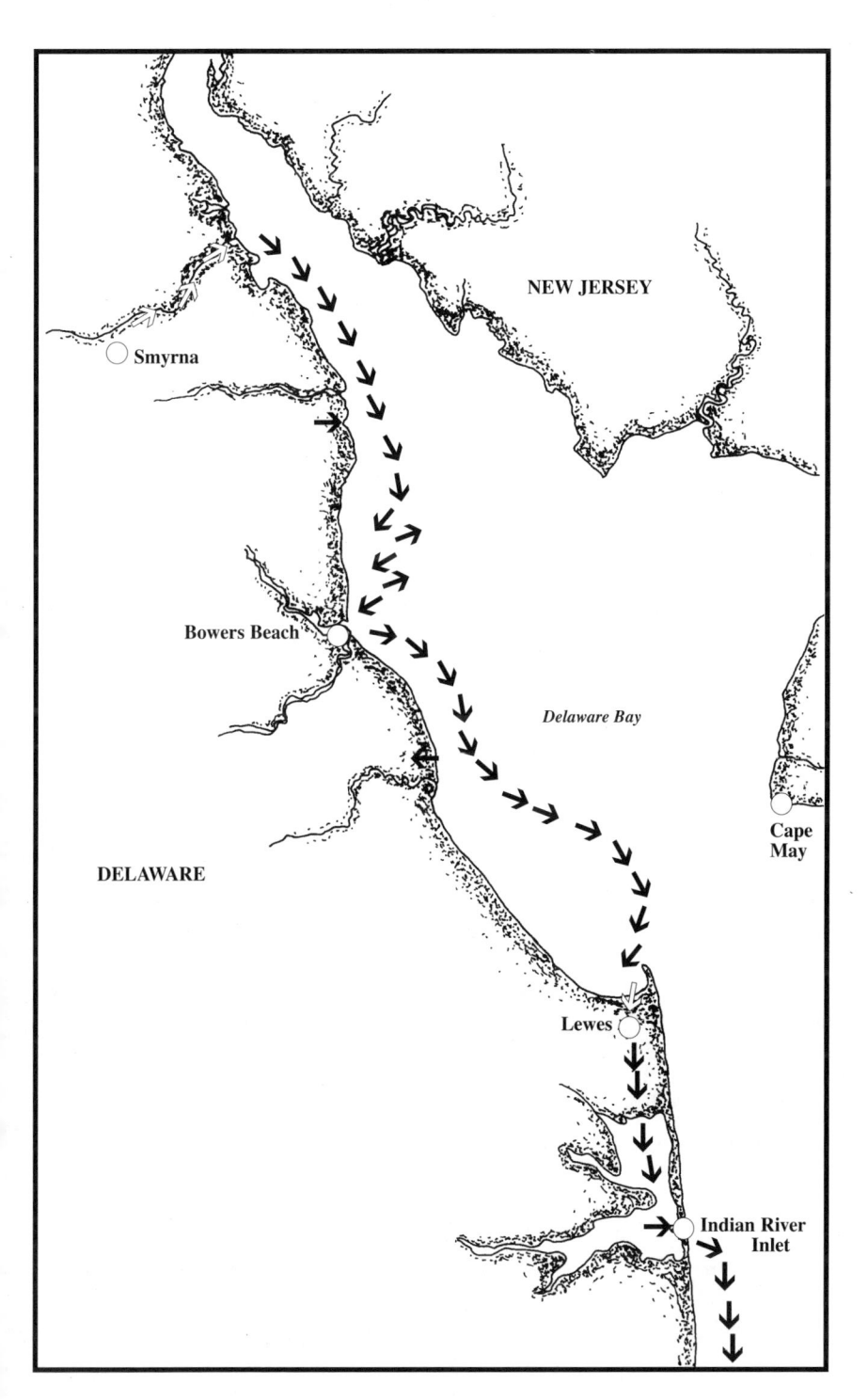

The Log of the Sherry D

The wind was blowing out of the northeast and was just right. I could set a course close hauled right down the Bay past Bombay Hook. I set the sails, shut off the motor and was taking it out of the well when there was a wind shift I had not noticed. The *Sherry D* jibed and the boom swung around and hit me in the head. Luckily it just skimmed the top of my head as that boom is a heavy thing. I think I was hit with the block that guided the main sheet, more than the boom, but it knocked my favorite khaki captain's hat into the water. I got a fat lip and chipped a tooth but nothing more serious. I was more concerned about my hat so I came about again, this time right on top of the cap and snatched it out of the water. This should mean a "good luck day" and we would see if this were so. The wind was playing tricks — first out of the south and then the southeast. I made good time however, due to the ebbing of the tide.

It's now past noon and I'm just southwest of Ship John Shoal Lighthouse. The *Sherry D* is again sailing herself. Time for lunch. It's getting hazy and Lewes is a long way off. I have to be prepared for anything, but so far, so good.

The wind has changed several times causing me to tack. The currents are favorable and are taking me south down the Delaware Bay. It is now 4:40 pm and the tides are starting to change. The wind is from the south and right on my nose. I sailed close to Bowers Beach just in case I had to get out of some bad weather then went back out to try for another tack. I was getting nowhere, and it was really getting hazy. The weather report called for thunderstorms with hail at the mouth of the Delaware Bay and Cape Henlopen late in the afternoon or early evening. I was still 20 miles from Lewes, and I decided then to chance running into Bowers Beach. There were some big boats and a lot of small ones bucking the waves on their way out to get their fish. I didn't know anything about Bowers Beach and Robert de Gast had passed this one up. I always had the impression that one of the bad things about the Delaware Bay was that there were few safe harbors to put into in case of bad weather. I had best take this one, as I knew if all those fishing boats could get in, then I could also.

I dropped the sails and motored in with the current. No problem. Fishing boats were lined up all around and I found myself a spot and docked. I was immediately approached by a man who informed me that I was in a chartered fishing boat's slip. He said I could tie up in front of his place and that he would help me (I readily accepted his help as the current was very strong now, much worse than at Smyrna.) This fellow tied me off to another fishing boat and I was told there was an eight-foot tide there and I could ride up and down with the fishing boat that was already tied for that rise and fall.

I learned later that this nice fellow was Pete Jensen. He owned the Crab Spot Restaurant which he and his wife had bought as a venture the year before. Pete is from Kent Island, Maryland and is head of the Department of Fisheries for Maryland (Department of Natural Resources). After a long chat, I offered to pay him for letting me tie up for the night. He declined my offer and said he would be pleased if I would eat in his restaurant.

The reason for my desire to make Lewes that evening was because it was Memorial Day weekend and my wife, Sherry, would be meeting me at the town dock there. We had pre-arranged this rendezvous and now I would be a day late. Since there was no way to contact each other directly, we had also pre-arranged for messages to be relayed to one another through our central home base. I, therefore, called home to leave the message, "I was in Bowers Beach, some 30 road-miles north of Lewes and would not be able to make Lewes tonight. If at all possible could she drive here and we would have dinner at the Crab Spot." I found that Sherry had called home ahead of me and that she had arrived in Lewes earlier during the day and was waiting for me there. If I didn't arrive by 8 pm, she would call home again to check on any messages from me. She had also taken a room in Ocean View, Delaware at Mrs. Quillan's very nice Bed and Breakfast. Unfortunately, that meant there would be no dinner together that night, but at least I left word for her to meet me at the town dock in Lewes between 5 pm and 6 pm the next day.

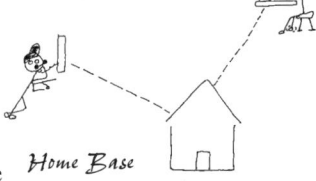

I met Pete Jensen again and we had a nice long talk while enjoying some very fine Kent Island-type crab cakes. I was interested in the ecology of the area and the environmental future of the Bay. I knew that Mr. Jensen was a real authority on this subject, in addition to his expertise in choice of crabs for his crab cakes. I also learned much about Bowers Beach, and the reason why all the locals came to look at my little boat. Pete Jensen told me that he had never seen a sailboat in there before.

Bowers Beach was another unusual find. It was first settled in the late 1600's at the mouth of the Murderkill River. The currents are the swiftest of any on the East Coast. This is due to the waters draining from the marshes of this narrow but deep cut that runs all the way up stream to Frederica. It also enters into the Delaware Bay at a point where the fast moving Delaware River enters into the wide part of the Bay. The tides can rise and fall some eight feet in a 5 to 7-hour period. I was told that one of the thoughts of how the river got its name was not from these treacherous currents, but from the original and Old English meaning of "Murder" being "Muddy" and "Kill" being a "Creek." Thus, the river, Muddy Creek, was named because the strong currents carried with them the rich muds from the marshes and wetlands inland. At the same time the currents were carrying the muds from inland to shoal in the Bay, they also carried the rich nutrients to feed the marine life, the reason for the good fishing grounds nearby.

I walked along the docks that night and watched the large head boats bring in their catches. (A head boat is a fishing boat that charges a fee per person to go out and fish, or so much per head.) Fish cleaners set up their cleaning booths and charge so much per fish to clean them. It was a good way for someone to go fishing and have his catch cleaned and packed in ice, ready for its trip home for dinner or freezer. The place was a beehive with Donovans Dock being a focal point.

My wife (being a Donovan) had worked with family history in this area and found Donovan land grants as far back as 1701 from William Penn.

Back from the dock was a large parking lot where even buses brought whole groups of people to go fishing and the drivers would wait till the boats returned. Bars and restaurants surrounded the area and I'm sure many of those stories of the "one that got away" were told over and over. Further on the other side of town was the Heartbreak Hotel.

After a walk around town I returned to the *Sherry D*, and found a large group of people gathered around looking down at her. There was nothing wrong other than the fact that I had to explain that she was just a visiting sailboat. One fellow, who worked on one of the large commercial fishing boats (and who had obviously had a little too much to drink), asked how I got here. When I told him about my trip and that I started just north of Annapolis, he looked at my little boat and then again at me; then said, "Man, you've got guts."

I was beginning to learn now, that the Delaware Bay was an interesting body of water. It was not just all business with its shipping lanes to ports north to Wilmington, Philadelphia, the New Jersey shores and to the C&D to Baltimore and the Chesapeake. But it offered much to the ecosystem — sanctuaries for birds and wildlife, as well as recreational opportunities for people. The Bombay Hook National Wildlife Refuge is located between the Smyrna River and Bowers Beach. I wished for more time to explore and study this interesting area.

The bad weather had passed me by without incident; I was another day late into my voyage, but I was glad that I had made the decision to go into Bowers Beach. I was tired. It had been another full and great day. I kept my clothes on, placed my good luck Captain's Cap on the shelf above, laid back on my bunk and thought about what tomorrow would bring. I hoped to leave on the outgoing tide, about 10 am in the morning.

Chapter 8

Day Seven - Bowers Beach to Lewes

Sunday - May 24th, 1987

It was another good night as I had slept hard right through all of the activity of the head boats coming in and going out at all hours. The *Sherry D* rode well with the tide as she was tied to the fishing boat alongside the dock. The weather still did not look good but it wasn't raining and I had another hour to pass before the start of ebb tide that I needed to carry me out of the mouth of the Murderkill River. I decided to have some breakfast at the Heartbreak Hotel and made my way the 3 to 4 blocks to the other side of town. This was another experience, as the hotel reminded me of something out of the past. The structure was a large older house with lots of old ornate trim around the roof line. It was probably very fashionable in its day, but now a 4 by 8 piece of plywood led to the entrance across the front porch. Inside, I almost fell through the floor due to the floorboards being so weak. The breakfast was good, however, and I enjoyed the

The Heartbreak Hotel.

experience. After breakfast, I returned to the boat, cleaned up, filled the water jugs and replenished the ice chest. The tide had changed and the current was picking up speed. I untied my lines, swung out into the current with motor running and made my way out of the Murderkill River, glad I had found Bowers Beach and was now on my way again.

No trouble getting out. I played the currents just right and headed on 60 degrees toward the entrance marker to Bowers Beach. It was hazy all around and the wind was light, out of the northeast. I went up on the foredeck to raise the sails and, by the time I got them up, it was socked in with fog. I couldn't even find the entrance marker. I swung around to 120 degrees and turned back to 60 degrees; the visibility was nil. I was committed and would never be able to get back to Bowers Beach against the current with my little motor. I decided to head on 60 degrees for another 15 minutes then tack on 150 degrees for 15 minutes and check my course again.

It was a good thing that I checked my compass prior to the fog's setting in. The 60 degree course brought me so close to the marker that I could see its image in the fog as I passed right by it. The fog began to lift and I saw the tower at Big Stone Beach and took my bearings; 150 degrees was a good course. My charts showed a good eight-foot depth all the way, but the wind was shifting now and I couldn't hold it. The *Sherry D* kept drifting to 180 degrees. I decided to head due east and really go out, as my speed was being cut trying to point up in order to stay offshore. If I could get out to Brandywine Shoal, I figured I could run on a reach to Lewes and gain ground for that incoming tide. This meant I had to go four to five miles out, set a course on 90 degrees, sail for one hour then change to 180 degrees. Visibility was great now. I could see the ships in the channel and the jetty off the Mispillion River. I was moving well and wanted to get to Lewes on that incoming tide by 4 pm.

What I failed to calculate was that the incoming tide to Lewes would also be the tide pushing up the Bay and against me. On my 180 degree course, I could see what I thought was Lewes way off; and, to the west I thought, was Broadkill Beach. I changed my course and headed inland toward Broadkill Beach. I later realized, after I took a bearing on what I thought was BWN "A", which actually was BWN "B" (black and white buoys used to mark channels), that I was two towns off course, about four miles north, and was heading for Fowlers Beach. Now all that time I spent running east was lost and I had to point up again. The tide was now hitting me and I needed speed in order to buck it. Otherwise, I would flounder. Out I went again on another tack. The wind really picked up and so did the waves. I was pushing because I had to get into Lewes before 5:30 pm to avoid the outgoing tide which would keep me from getting in the Roosevelt Inlet and to the Lewes Rehoboth Canal.

As I swung around in that chop, my sails got out of control; and I was flying the big genoa. I fell backward, hit the tiller and broke the end right off where I had my steering lines tied. I noticed also a small rip in the clue of the mainsail. All I could think of was how hard I had worked on that tiller and how beautiful it had looked with its many coats of varnish. Now I was sailing with half a tiller and had to retie my steering lines. With only a rough stick to hang onto, I continued to sail.

Finally, I saw the entrance to Roosevelt Inlet. The waves were rough, but I needed to keep the sails up for speed. I did manage to get the motor in the well but kept it running in neutral in case I needed it. I was moving so fast that I let her go in under sail. On my way in I saw a lot of people fishing along the jetty; they waved and clapped as I pulled in the sails to make the turn into the Canal. I was only a stone's throw from them and apparently they had been watching me for some time. I'm sure that from where they sat it appeared that my little boat raised up on top of a swell and then disappeared as she went down into the trough.

I found the Delaware not a bad bay to sail. I expected much worse and kept looking for it. It was only at the mouth, when I was bucking the tide and heavy winds, that I realized the Delaware was showing me her ugly teeth. She was not going to let me go through without taking a bite. She did get my tiller.

I sailed up the Lewes and Rehoboth Canal and was at the bridge at exactly 5:30 pm, just three minutes before the tide ebbed. My wife, Sherry, was there waving and motioned for me to go over to the city dock across the canal. With sails down and motor running, I had to make several passes in order to position myself. The tide was starting to run heavy now.

Tomorrow I would go through the canal to Rehoboth Bay and the Indian River Inlet. It was a great day, a nice sail, my wife was there to greet me, and once again the *Sherry D* came through like a pro. What more could I ask for?

Hi, Honey. I'm here!

Chapter 9

Day Eight - Lewes to Indian River Inlet

Monday - May 25th, 1987

It was really a treat getting my feet dry again. Both Sherrys looked great. We had a good dinner in Lewes. Met Sherry's friend Olga, who was the hostess at the new restaurant across from the city dock and whose husband owned the large headboat that was docked there. Then we drove to Ocean View, near Bethany Beach, to a bed and breakfast, run by Mrs. Quillen, where Sherry had rented a room. Mrs. Quillen was the retired postmistress of Ocean View. It was Memorial Day and very crowded at the resort areas.

We slept well and awoke with a full day ahead of us. We placed my dirty clothes in the laundromat while having breakfast in Bethany, and then checked out the Marina at Indian River Inlet. We found it to be completely rebuilt since we had been there five or six years ago. The manager of the marina was a very nice young fellow and after he learned of my trip, in which he was interested, he invited me to bring the *Sherry D* in and tie up at the end slip without charge. Of course I accepted his generous offer with pleasure, but couldn't understand the "no charge." He replied, "Don't worry about it, we'll get you later." I couldn't imagine what he meant, other than the fact that I might like it so much there, that I'd buy one of the large pleasure boats docked there and rent a slip from him for life. I certainly thanked him with a smile.

We went to check the Indian River Inlet. It looked like "Hell's Gate." I was glad I wasn't going out until tomorrow morning, hoping it would be better on an ebb tide. We then drove into Rehoboth and checked with the drawbridge tender. He said it would be no trouble to open the bridge. I was concerned with the delay it would cause the holiday travelers, but the bridge tender assured me that he would take care of it and not to worry. He was helpful in pointing out some shallow spots in the canal. Other than those, I should have no problem. I told him that I would be coming through about 2:30 pm, as that would be when the tide started to flood in Lewes. I made the same inquiry at the bridge in Lewes and was given an "OK." All was going great, except I miscalculated on the changing tides, I was about an hour off. I filled my gas tank, and then it was time to go.

It was 3 pm when I started out. Sherry would follow by car. She would stop and check me out at the bridges. I calculated my new ETA at Indian River Inlet to be 8 pm. Everything went like clockwork; the bridge tenders were perfect, and I moved right through with each giving me a "good-bye/good luck" wave. At one point I did scrape bottom but went right through the soft mud. I turned and waved to the tender to signal that I was OK and went on under motor.

The wind had really picked up when I hit Rehoboth Bay. I raised the sails and flew across. It was an easy course to follow, until I went through the Long Neck Inlet. There was a non-working dredge sitting right in the channel and I saw no markers other than the dredge's danger floats. I came in close, and "wham!" I was hard aground. I tried everything but couldn't budge her off. I thought help was near when several power boats started in, but when they saw this tired ole sailor, they just turned around. Apparently, they must have thought it was too shallow for them also. Finally, a young man with his three sons came by in a heavy runabout, threw me a line and, in no time, had us off. He knew the channel and where it was shoaling, so he called to me to follow his wake.

On the other side of Long Neck, I turned toward the Indian River Inlet. The tide was coming in and the wind was blowing a gale right over my nose. A cloud cover hovered just beneath the evening sky and the temperature began to drop. It was down now in the low 50's. The wind-chill factor made it feel like 30 degrees.

Draw Bridge at Lewes.

I was freezing and the only thing that saved me was a wool sweatshirt with a hood that Sherry insisted I buy in Lewes. I had been warm during the day and we were coming into summer. "Why did I need an expensive thing like that" I had thought, but gave into the argument. I had been wearing my foul-weather jacket which normally would have checked the coldness. Now I took the foul-weather jacket off, donned the wool sweatshirt and put the jacket back on over my sweatshirt, but I was still cold.

I was now motoring all the way. I barely moved. Much to my surprise, I was in and tied up at the floating docks by 7:30 pm. Sherry arrived at the same time. I was cold, beat and hungry, so I quickly jumped in Sherry's car and headed for the Magnolia Restaurant in Ocean View for a steak dinner. Then, a last night at Mrs. Quillen's.

The Inland Waterway between Rehoboth and Rehoboth Bay.

CHAPTER 10

Day Nine – Indian River Inlet to Ocean City Inlet

Tuesday - May 26th, 1987

Back at the *Sherry D* early in the morning, I reflected on the events of the previous day. I thought it was a wonderful Memorial Day. I hated to say good-bye to my wife. I so wished she could stay longer, but she had to get back to work. I calculated that I would run out on the ebb tide about 8:30 am, but now my thoughts were "maybe later and maybe not at all." The weather forecast was bad, 10 to 15 knot winds, easterly, three to five-foot waves, with rain and this would be my first ocean experience — plus, tomorrow's forecast was even worse. There appeared to be no relief until Thursday and I wanted to be in Wachapreague by Friday, another possible delay in the trip. I decided to get everything ready to go if that was my decision. There was an electrical outlet on the dock next to the boat, so I took advantage of this to charge my batteries. I sewed my torn sail and rounded off the rough edges on my broken tiller. I filled the stove and lantern with the last of my kerosene and washed down the *Sherry D*. Then, I went over to the marina for a quick breakfast.

The sun came out and the wind settled down. It was now 8:30 am — time to make that decision. I decided to check with the Coast Guard station, which was right next door. Their reports were no different from what I had previously heard and they suggested that, should I decide to go, to hold off another hour to allow the tide to fall another foot. The bridge had a 35-foot clearance normally at high tide, but because of all the run-off from the heavy rains, it was about four feet above normal. I needed 32 feet. However, the longer I waited past slack tide and once the ebb really started, the rougher the inlet would be. There was a deep

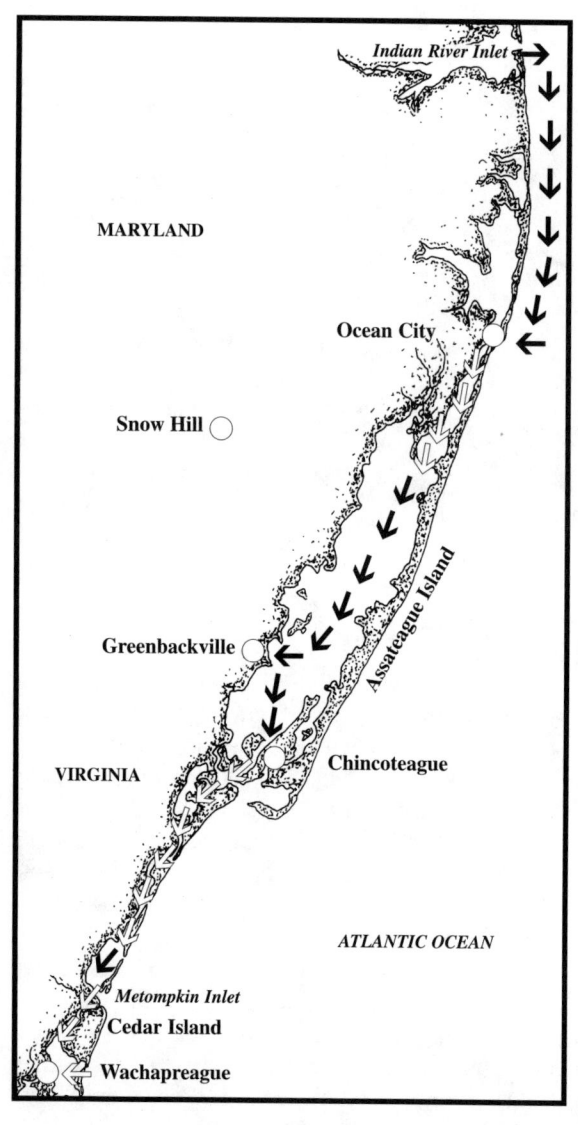

90-foot hole right at the entrance; and when that water starts to move, it pours right in that hole, causing a swirling turmoil.

I walked over to the inlet, stood on the bridge and looked over the ocean. It was beautiful, with the sun out, but black to the northeast and hazy elsewhere. The wind had calmed, not much wave and the inlet was at the end of the slack; the tide was just beginning to move out. It was a piece of cake — "Go for it." It was now 9:15 am and I stopped by the Coast Guard Station to file for a flight plan on my way back to the boat. They asked that I call them when I got to Ocean City. As I walked back to the boat, the sun would come out and then haze over. I didn't know if it was the good Lord or the devil who was urging me on. I guess I wouldn't know until the end of this trip.

At 10:15 am, I was motoring out of the marina entrance into Rehoboth Bay and at 10:30 am I was going through the inlet. I slowed the motor as I went under the bridge. I prayed for enough clearance. As I looked up, I was sure the top of my mast would hit, but it must have cleared by at least two to three feet (I could have a 100-foot clearance and still it would look like it would hit.) I started picking up speed under the bridge and the swells were bigger on the other side. The wind was starting to blow on my nose pretty hard, but the current was taking me through. I saw white water in front of me — oh, no! That damn hole! The *Sherry D* was riding pretty good however, and I gave more throttle but held back about

I walked over to the inlet, stood on the bridge and looked over the ocean. The wind had calmed, not much wave and the inlet was at the end of the slack. The tide was just beginning to move out. It was a piece of cake, "Go for it."

I could have had a 100-foot clearance and still it would look like it would hit.

two notches, in case I needed it later. There was no way that I could turn around and go back now. I sat in the hatchway to get a better balance to the boat and it also gave me something to hang onto. I wore a life jacket but not the safety harness; I was ready for the turbulence and steered by the steering lines.

At the end of the jetty where the white water churned, the fast moving current poured down into that 90-foot hole, followed by the ocean waves that broke over the top. My bow went under, the stern went up, and the motor spun like a Mixmaster out of the water. Then the motor dug in as the bow lifted almost straight up. I looked above, and the mast appeared to be laying horizontally over my head. Just when I thought the *Sherry D* was about to do a back flip, down went the bow into the white water again and the boat rolled from side to side. I thought the devil was surely pulling me down in that damn hole and I prayed for the Good Lord to pull me back up.

We were starting to make headway now, but the wind began to blow harder on the nose. Finally, I was through it, and the choppy waves turned to ocean swells with the traditional 30-foot trough. The forecast was right, four to five-

Uh-oh!

The Log of the Sherry D

At the end of the jetty where the white water churned, the fast-moving current poured down into that 90-foot hole.

foot wave heights. I motored out past Can #1, the entrance marker to the Indian River Inlet, about one-half mile out. The *Sherry D* would ride down in the trough of those swells, come up and kind of wiggle as she raised her bow. I had the strange feeling that she was laughing and saying to me "Well, ole boy, we did that one, didn't we?" It was time to raise the sails. Everything was pre-rigged and should have been easy except for the bouncing around and the wind. I secured the safety harness, as I didn't wear it through the inlet because I wanted to be free to swim away had anything happened to the boat. I was rigged for the working jib, as I was expecting some heavy weather later; and I sure didn't want to change a head sail again, especially out in that ocean. I made my way up to the bow and ran up the jib to luff in the breeze. Then, I hung tight to the mast and quickly raised the main. Back in the cockpit, I close-hauled and sheeted home the sails, then cut off the motor. I put the tiller down hard, the sails filled and the little boat heeled gently on a port tack. We were a good two miles out to sea and white water churned in our wake as we headed on an easy due southerly course. I shivered with excitement; the salt winds brought the blood to my brow and made my stomach flutter.

The *Sherry D* and I were the only ones out here on the surface of the sea. I was in control now and I felt good about myself and my boat. It appeared to me that this trip was not as I had intended, but more like one of man against the elements. I was doing nicely as a loner and I wondered now, that if I had someone else with me, would I take these chances? Would a discussion change my inclinations? I felt sure that if someone else had been with me, that I would have aborted this trip the first day when I crossed the mouth of the Chester River.

It was now 10:40 am. The winds veered more to the northeast and began to slack a little. The ocean smoothed out and I let the sails out a little to continue my southerly course on a reach. The sun came out bright and beautiful and once again I felt the Good Lord was certainly on my side. An hour later we were passing Bethany Beach. I could see the large Sea Colony Condominium on the coast line. I marked off six miles on the chart, and in another hour we were passing the Fenwick Island Lighthouse. Another six miles and then the Gold Coast. I was about two miles out and came in on a broad reach to take some pictures. It was a beautiful sail and it was turning out to be a pretty day. This ocean sail was a piece of cake compared to what I have been through before. I wanted one for the record, however, just to prove I was out here. So, I set my camera on the cabin top, as we sailed along so smoothly. I set the camera on timed setting and in the 10-second period before it clicked, I jumped back to the cockpit and grabbed the tiller in time to include myself in the picture. The Ferris wheel at south Ocean City is in sight now. I'm way ahead of schedule and will see how it turns out as I have to go in the Ocean City Inlet on a flood tide. The Coast Guard warned me that the Ocean City Inlet was pretty bad also.

At 3:30 pm, I made a pass under sail close to the inlet to check it out. The wind really came up strong again from the northeast and caused some large swells as I was much closer to shore now. A few small boats were trying to make their way out but were having a hard time as waves were crashing in against them. I decided not to chance it with the sails up, even through it did cross my mind that I had much more power with sails and the wind was favorable. I just didn't want to push my luck any more. I came about and ran back out close hauled, cut her into the wind and put the motor back in the well, harnessed up and headed to the foredeck to lower the sails. It was rough and we bounced around, but had no trouble. I'm getting used to this now, and I have a system while wrapping myself around the mast.

I set the camera on timed setting and before it clicked, I jumped back to the cockpit and grabbed the tiller in time for the picture.

When I returned to the cockpit, I discovered that my AM/FM radio bracket had broken loose from the hinges, the boom chock had split, and one of the fair leads had pulled out. Things were breaking up pretty fast in the strong winds, but no real damage and nothing that couldn't be fixed. My sewing job on the main sail had held.

With motor only, I started in with a following sea. I made the approach to the inlet, past the Ferris wheel and all the amusements. If I could sell tickets for my ride, I would make a fortune. It was like riding a roller coaster. I had no problems and rode right in with the motor. Actually, I could have sailed in and that would have been great. As soon as I got to calm water, a large power boat from Biscayne, Florida came plowing in and her wake was worse than any of the ocean waves. The captain had no concern for me or my boat, causing us to almost capsize. This captain didn't even give us the courtesy of a hand wave. I guess I'm back in the real world again.

In any event, by 4:30 pm I was anchored behind the Ocean City Inlet by the bridge, in calm water. The tide is starting to move in fast now. At 6 pm, my anchor appeared to be holding well. It was another interesting day, and I'm glad I gambled. I called the Coast Guard in Ocean City and asked them to relay to the Indian River Inlet station that I made it and my thanks. Now it is all behind me and tomorrow I start a new adventure through the barrier islands and the marshes. Tomorrow is Assateague. They are still calling for rain and bad weather until Thursday but with temperatures in the 90's. It is 58 degrees right now.

It's time for a Rusty Nail, a little dinner on board, and then to hit the bunk — I've earned it. What a day!

Back in the real world.

Chapter 11

Day Ten - Ocean City to Chincoteague

Wednesday - May 27th, 1987

I awoke after a good night's sleep, to a beautiful, sunny morning. For a moment, I thought I had overslept. The sun was a welcome sight and inspired me to get up and prepare for my early departure. The weather report was still calling for cloudy, plus rain showers with warmer temperatures (it was now 58 degrees.) After washing and dressing, I made breakfast (had to use up all perishables as ice had run out.) The tide appeared to be slackening, it was time to go.

At 9:30 am, I motored out. Everything was working well. The current was just right and I headed for the Assateague Channel, passing the Ocean City commercial fishing docks. I had no idea that Ocean City supported such a commercial fleet. I set up my little nav-station on the hatchway cover. It was an easy course, well-marked, and I could see the Sandy Point Bridge to Assateague five and a half miles ahead. The chart showed a 38-foot clearance, which was no problem for me since the *Sherry D* needed only a 32-foot clearance.

It was such a pretty day, I decided to spend some time snapping pictures. When I was under the bridge, I raised the mainsail. It was a good thing I did because I started to skim the bottom. I pulled in on the main and heeled over slightly. We went right through the soft mud. I decided I needed a depth finder so I dropped my centerboard one foot. If it hit again, I'd pull it up. As I passed under the bridge, looking up at the mast, I noticed that, in my haste to depart, I had forgotten to take down the anchor light. I needed the anchor light for two more nights and I had no reserve kerosene left on board. After removing the lantern, I was somewhat relieved to see that it had plenty of kerosene left in its reservoir. I had charged my batteries at Indian River, so I had plenty of electrical power if needed.

By noon, I was rounding marker "39". I was through the channel and now in Chincoteague Bay, a wide expanse of water. I could see my next marker way off, but it was beginning to haze. My compass reading indicated that I was on a 210 degree course. Fortunately, the temperature was beginning to rise and it was getting very warm.

At 1:30 pm the wind started to pick up. The Chincoteague Bay is an easy body of water to sail, however it is imperative to follow the markers, as it is very shallow. It started to get cold again and the wind really began to blow. The main was the only sail up with a following sea. We were moving fast enough and ahead of schedule.

We crossed the Maryland line at 3 pm, and Greenbackville was just off to starboard. I decided to pass it up and headed right for Chincoteague. If things went as well as they had been, I could make up a whole day. Compared to what we had been through so far, this was a little boring. The sail was too easy. It looked dark over Chincoteague, however, and I could feel the devil beckoning his evil finger again. We'd see what would happen.

It was 5 pm and I had no trouble entering Chincoteague. Sailed right into the narrow channel that separates the town from the marshes and mainland. Chincoteague is actually an island and may be considered one of the barriers, other than the fact that it lies just behind the barrier island of Assateague and is separated by Assateague Channel.

I was able to come in alongside the bulkhead of R&R Boat Rentals about 500 yards north of the swing bridge that separates the town from the marshes. R&R is owned by a nice young family, Bill Hensen, his wife and their little daughter. They not only rent small fishing boats with outboards, they also have a little store specializing in the basics, but mostly in fishing tackle. They also sell gas and ice and have a few motel rooms for visiting and vacationing sport fishermen.

I had been warned before my voyage that Chincoteague was not hospitable towards sailors and that it was a fisherman's town. This I found to be only half correct. Yes, it was a fisherman's town, but, as a sailor, I couldn't have been treated better. The Hensens didn't even want to charge me dockage and they were helpful with tidal information and suggestions about what to do in Chincoteague. While we talked, an older fellow stopped to check into the motel. I found that he worked for C&P Telephone Company and lived not far away from my home. Art, as he introduced himself, explained that he came to this place each year for his one-week vacation. He had been doing this for years and loved to fish. He didn't care if he caught anything or not; he just liked to get out on the water. He carried his own outboard in the back of his station wagon and rented only the boat. He had found that Chincoteague was the best place for a quick get-away. He could really relax there, and since he comes to the same place, fishes in the same spots, eats in the same restaurants, etc., he saves a lot of time for such a short vacation. For Art, I thought that to be good planning.

After his check-in, Art invited me to drive with him to his favorite restaurant, Pony Pines. This we did and had a great meal.

I had an old friend, Norine Fox, who recently moved to Chincoteague. Norine was a retired school librarian who was associated with my wife in the Anne Arundel County, Maryland, school system and is a good friend of ours. So after dinner, I gave Norine a call to tell her I finally arrived. She and Ray picked me up at the R&R Boat Rental store and then introduced me to their new home. Of course, a good dessert was waiting, which we ate while Norine told me about Chincoteague and Assateague. Norine, being a retired librarian, did her homework well. She was a regular visitor to Assateague Island and to the National Wildlife Refuge. In anything she does, Norine is the type that always obtains and retains a wealth of information and I appreciated her sharing this with me.

Assateague Island

I thought it interesting when she told me that Assateague Island was divided into three major areas, each having its own management under different governing bodies. At the north end of the island is the Assateague State Park. These 680 acres are owned by the State of Maryland and are managed by the Maryland Department of Natural Resources as a state park. On the south, in Virginia, is the Chincoteague National Wildlife Refuge. This refuge, managed by the U.S. Fish and Wildlife Service, is the prime Atlantic flyway habitat and is essential to the survival of many native and migratory species, ranging from Canada geese to Monarch butterflies. More than 200 species of birds, as well as wild ponies, may be found in the refuge. The Chincoteague National Wildlife Refuge is so named as the Federal Government normally names such places, by the name of the nearest town. It was purchased in 1943 by the Federal Government with Duck Stamp revenues, for the sole purpose of protecting this valuable property for wildlife.

The third area is the Assateague Island National Seashore. It encompasses the entire circumference of Assateague Island and is managed by the National Park Service. Together, these agencies hold in trust a priceless seashore heritage of wildlands, wildlife, and outdoor recreation for the public.

In a way, the town of Chincoteague and the resources of Assateague Island are similar. They each depend on one another. Assateague Island provides living quarters only for wildlife and Chincoteague provides the same for us humans. Chincoteague is a peaceful little town with nice shops, restaurants and older homes. Though it supports a great number of the tourists who visit the sites at Assateague, it is also active in commercial and sport fishing. Sleepy in the off season, Chincoteague comes alive with a hustle and bustle in the tourist season. The annual wild pony round-up the last week in July and its auction supporting the Volunteer Fire Department are its highlights.

CHAPTER 12

Day Eleven - Chincoteague to Folly Creek

Thursday - May 28th, 1987

THE GOOD OLE BOYS

I was up, washed and dressed by 6 am. The fishing fleet had started out at 4:30 am and there was no sleeping after that. I wanted to be at the south end of the island by 8:45 am when the tide would be coming in the inlet. I was hoping to ride the currents through on a rising tide to get behind Wallops Island and through the shallows. I was sure that it would be touch and go.

To save time, I decided to eat out for breakfast. Don's Restaurant was just a few blocks down Main Street towards the bridge. After breakfast, the waitress was kind enough to fill my thermos with coffee. I telephoned Norine to thank her for her hospitality and asked her to call Sherry and ask her to bring me some more "Skin So Soft" when she came to meet me in Wachapreague. I was down to less than a fourth of a bottle now and found that "Skin So Soft" really did a great job in keeping the mosquitoes away and it smelled pretty good too. (Me with no bath!)

I found the trick to having the swing bridge open, as I had been warned that the tender would go off and leave the bridge unattended. This was not really so. There was a small Bridge Tender's Shack with a CB and marine radio at the other end of the bridge and that was where he would stay when there was no traffic. I walked across the bridge to talk to this fellow eye to eye and to be sure the bridge would open for me. He seemed to be a nice enough fellow and told me that he had seen my little blue boat from the bridge. When I was ready to come through, I was to just give him a call on the radio. He added he "weren't leave'n the comfort o' that shack until he see'd me acomin'." We understood each other and we parted with a handshake and a smile. After seeing the bridge tender's shack and then taking special note, on my way back across the bridge, of the little control booth this fellow had to sit in while opening the bridge, I appreciated his wanting to spend his spare time at the shack.

When I returned to the *Sherry D*, I noticed a water faucet about 50 yards from the boat and decided to top off my 10-gallon water tank. To my surprise, Norine and Ray had come to see me off and Norine gave me a new bottle of "Skin So Soft" of her own. (No one could understand how much I appreciated that unless he had sailed through those marshes behind the barrier islands.)

It was now 7:45 am, the tide was slack and it was time to go. I walked Norine and Ray to their car and we said our goodbyes. Then I stopped by R&R boat rentals to once again thank the Hensons for their kindness and wish them much success in their new-found endeavor. Back at the boat, I radioed the bridge tender and started the motor. I had previously untied and stowed all the lines except the stern line. I gave it a flick as the bow turned out toward mid-stream and I started toward the bridge, but did not see the bridge tender. As I approached, I saw him come out of his shack and slowly walk to the control booth. At just the right moment, he had the traffic stopped and the bridge began to swing open. The *Sherry D* glided right through. I gave the tender a blast on my fog horn to signify that I was through and to close the bridge. I looked around, and there were Ray and Norine taking pictures of me and waving farewell. I moved in close along the bulkhead and shouted another "Thanks for everything."

It was now a little after 8 am and I was a good half hour ahead of schedule. When I reached the Chincoteague Inlet, the tide was just beginning to push in. This was perfect, the sun came out bright, and the sportfishing boats were all over the channel. I had a great time maneuvering through them while asking how the fishing was going. No one seemed to care that the fish were not biting, it was just a great day to be out on the water. I looked for Art, but decided he was sleeping his vacation away. It looked like it would continue to be a beautiful day. We would see what new adventures lay ahead.

I was now leaving Chincoteague and going behind Wallops Island. This was the start of the VIP (Virginia Inside Passage). The tide was running strong and, with my little motor running half throttle, I moved right along. The water, however, appeared to be another "slick ca'm" as there was no wind. Bend after bend, turn after turn, it was the Smyrna River all over again, but this time without sails. The Wallops Island Tracking Station and Rocket Range took up much of the landscape. I wanted to sail so badly as I kept remembering what a thrill that was on the Smyrna. In the distance, I could see the Wallops Island Bridge across the marsh. The chart showed a clearance of 40 feet, but now scaffolding was hanging down and men were working on the bridge. As I made the last turn to the approach, I saw the center span was clear and I went under with no trouble. One of the workmen called to the others and shouted, "That's a sailboat." About that time, a little breeze came up and I raised the main only and kept the motor

I was now leaving Chincoteague and going behind Wallops Island. This was the start of the VIP (Virginia Inside Passage). It was a beautiful day. I laid my chart on the cabin top along with my navigation items and identification book, and chalked off the markers as I cruised along.

running. Work stopped on the bridge for awhile, and I wondered if that crew had ever seen a sailboat before.

The centerboard was down about one foot, as I used that for my depth finder — a little trick I learned from Robert de Gast. It worked well, as I did scrape bottom a few times, even though the tide was near high; I just pulled the board up and kept going. Crab pots were everywhere. More turns, more bends and more crab pots. I couldn't believe how fast and nicely I was moving through the water. I sat in the companionway again and steered by the steering lines. The chart was on the hatch cover, and I crossed off the markers as I passed them. It was an easy course to follow, so I did not need my compass. A few turns led to guesswork as the canal branched off in some places and I really couldn't see the next marker. I wasn't sure which branch to take, it was like flipping a coin. I made it through, however, and before long I was sailing straight across Kegotank Bay. I turned off the motor, stowed it in the lazarette, and raised the genoa. It was a great sail.

I tried taking pictures of the birds perched on the piling but they would fly on ahead of me just before I came within picture-taking range. This became a little game we would play. Once I killed the motor, thinking I could sneak up on them but they were way ahead of me and off they flew. It was a great way to pass the time.

It was now 11:30 am and I was nearing the southeast side of the Kegotank Bay when I saw a large black ship come through the marsh. At least I originally thought it to be the marsh. When I checked my chart I realized I was nearing the

Gargathy Inlet of the south end of Assawoman Island. The ship was coming from the ocean side through the inlet. Inside, it turned in my direction and I saw the red stripe running diagonally down her bow. It was a Coast Guard vessel, kind of stubby, and I subconsciously checked to see if I had my life jacket and fire extinguisher on board. She passed me by and continued on the same route that I just followed. I wondered how she would get through since I had touched bottom on several occasions. I never saw her again and assumed she just plowed her way through (maybe that's how they open the channel), or she is stuck in there to this day. I heard the ocean crashing on the other side of the dunes and it hit me, this is where Robert de Gast beached the *Slick Ca'm* and jumped off onto the shore. It was near lunch time and I thought what a great place to take a noontime break.

I turned into the sandy beach and ran the bow aground, threw the anchor ashore, tied it off and jumped over into the sand behind it, just as Robert de Gast had done 13 years previously. I had already played out a lot of line and just dug the anchor into the sand about 10 yards up on the beach. I climbed back on board without even getting my feet wet, lowered and furled the sails, and then went below to get some provisions for lunch. With lunch and camera in tow, I jumped back on the beach.

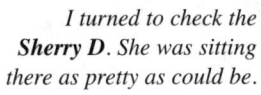

*I turned to check the **Sherry D**. She was sitting there as pretty as could be.*

It was a sight to see. The gulls and sandpipers ran all over the beach in front of me, picking at shells.

The sun glistened on the small waves rolling up on the beach with its shells and crystal-like sand.

I had heard about these horseshoe crab graveyards, where these crustaceans went to die after they laid their eggs.

    I walked over the dunes to the seaside. It was a sight to see. The ocean was right there. I turned to check on the *Sherry D*, and she was sitting there pretty as could be with the marshes in the background. It was picture taking time.
    I found an old driftwood plank and sat my lunch down on it. There was not a cloud in the sky. It was warm and a light breeze was blowing from the ocean. Gulls and sandpipers ran all over the beach in front of me picking at shells and appeared to be enjoying each other's company. The sun glistened on the small waves rolling up on the beach with its crystal-like sand. In my travels all over the world, I don't think that I have ever seen a more beautiful setting than this. I took picture after picture as I walked the beach with the birds, the sun and the breeze. Surely I was in heaven. It occurred to me that I could have been pulled down in that "damn hole" off the Indian River Inlet and now was reincarnated and returned as Robinson Crusoe. I was walking this beautiful beach with nothing but the birds, the salt air, the sun, the sand and the ocean for company. Up in the tall grass in the dunes, I found an area with hundreds of dead horseshoe crabs — large

ones, small ones, old ones and new ones. I had heard about these horseshoe crab graveyards, where these crustaceans went to die after they laid their eggs and, now, I was visiting one. This, coupled with my previous thoughts, led me to believe how wise they were to pick such a wonderful place to spend their eternal life. With this solemn thought, I turned and walked back to the beach. I saw Wallops Island satellite towers on the other side of the dunes and once again was brought back to the real world.

Low tide on Assawoman Island..

Oh, well.

After eating my lunch, I headed for the *Sherry D* to get my log book. I wanted to record my thoughts and impressions. This feeling was too good to lose. To my surprise, the tide was going out and the *Sherry D* was on the bottom. There was no way to get her off now. Oh well, if I had to be stuck, I couldn't think of a better place to be. I was only seven to 10 miles from Folly Creek where I had planned to spend the night. It was mid-afternoon and the tide should start back in about 4:30 pm. I was more than happy to wait it out.

About this time, a couple of fellows came by in a small runabout and offered to help me off. We tried, but there was just nothing we could do to get the *Sherry D* off, except wait for the tide to come in again. They indicated that they were just killing time, enjoying the sun and the beautiful day while occasionally trying their hands at fishing. They offered me a beer while we chatted, and then they said they would go to a spot around the bend and fish until the tide started in. They said they would be back and promised to help. We said our good-byes, I thanked them for the beer and watched them leave, never expecting to see them again. With this thought, I took my notebook and headed back to my lovely spot and proceeded to record my thoughts.

Much to my surprise, a few hours later my "foolin' and fishin' " friends returned. As promised, they had not forgotten me. I felt I should explain my surprise at seeing them because in this day and age everyone seems to be on his own. I had witnessed this before — it is not often that others are concerned for the welfare and safety of someone else. I had been brought up on the water and taught that everyone had a responsibility to help others in need. It was an understood tradition and the unwritten law of the sea, that everyone looked out for each other. Fortunately for me, these guys were from the old school. Later as we talked and I thanked them for returning, one of them said to me, "Why, hell, if we had been stuck out here, we'd of hoped that someone would help us." Yes, we had come from the same school. Even though I probably could have floated off myself with the tide, it was gratifying to know that there were still some "Good Ole Boys" around.

The tide had not quite come in enough and the *Sherry D* was still hard aground. We waited and talked and got to know each other. They were interested in my trip and one had read Robert de Gast's book. Both were from Pocomoke and insisted that I sail and see the Pocomoke River when I came around on the Bay side. They mapped out a plan and would hear of nothing else. I was to call them when I came up the Chesapeake. They had a friend who lived on the Pocomoke River about four miles up. He owned a large brick house and had a nice dock with white pilings. I was to look for it on the right once I passed Shelltown.

Their friend, I was told, liked sailboats and would be very disappointed if I didn't tie up at his dock. The owner, their friend, might not be there, however, as he lived in Philadelphia, but that was okay, they would meet me there. I learned that they were not fishermen. Van Wilkerson was a chicken farmer and his parents owned the Eastern Shoreman Restaurant on Route 13, just south of Pocomoke City. Van claimed that the Eastern Shoreman served the best crab cakes on the Shore. They would treat me to dinner. Jim Dykes was a dairy farmer and ran a very large and modern dairy farm on the Shore. I would also get a tour of the farm, in addition to a tour in Jim's runabout up the Pocomoke River to save time. This I couldn't pass up, and I recorded their names and phone numbers.

The tide was almost in now, and we pushed the stern off into deeper water. I jumped aboard while Van and Jim pushed the bow off. The *Sherry D* was picked up by the current and I started the motor. Jim and Van jumped into their boat and followed me to be sure I was okay. There was a nice breeze and I let the motor run while I went up on the foredeck to raise my sails. The *Sherry D* moved right out and Jim had to speed up his motor to keep up. They couldn't get over the fact that I was sailing. Jim maneuvered alongside while Van held up a big bluefish that

The "Good Ole Boys" wave good-bye.

they had caught and offered it to me for dinner. I had to refuse as my hands were too full with sailing to stop and clean a fish. I think they understood. We reached a fork in the channel, and they saw that I had my little boat under control. Jim and Van turned off waving a cheerful good-bye. I knew that I had made some new friends and I would meet these "Good Ole Boys" again.

I was doing nicely under sail and turned the motor off. I had just passed buoy 66 and "VABOOM," I was hard in the mud. Fortunately, the tide was still rising but it had not come up enough for me to get through this shallow part. I took the sails down and just let her sit there. This was a good time to finish putting my screens together. In about 30 minutes screens were together, and the tide was raising me off the bottom. I could feel the movement and started the motor again. I was off but this time without sails. This was one of those places between inlets where the currents don't know which way to flow. It depends on which current has the most force, and all the marsh knows is that the tide is rising. Now the current was against me and my little motor was straining. I only had a few hours of daylight left and I didn't want to be caught in the marsh after dark. At one point, however, I passed a marker and a very large osprey flew off his nest with a beautiful sunset in the background. He circled and landed in his nest again. It was one beautiful picture, and I had to go back.

Time was a factor now, but I decided to sacrifice and got my camera out. I made a wide turn, hoping I wouldn't go out of the channel, then headed back to the marker. The osprey took off as before and I snapped the shutter. The sun, however, had gone down behind the woods in the distance and the shot wasn't that good. Fifteen minutes of my precious time was gone. I thought I would never get through Metompkin Bay and then finally, with just enough daylight left, I was in Folly Creek. Where would I anchor? I had been to nearby Cedar Island many times before and I knew there was a dock out there and some large houses were being built on the north end of the island. I wondered if I had enough light left to make it. What could I lose? So, off I went. In no time, I was there and tied up at the "No Trespassing" dock just inside the inlet with the ocean not 500 feet from the dock. If anyone objected, they would have to tell me to move. I was tired and hungry. The little stove heated up quickly and I had dinner. After doing the dishes and putting things in order, I was ready for the sack. Tomorrow I would get up early and walk the beach to see the new development before heading to Wachapreague.

Cedar Island

Sherry D *tied to the "No Trespassing" dock at Cedar Island.*

CHAPTER 13

Days Twelve, Thirteen & Fourteen Cedar Island Dock to Wachapreague

Friday, Saturday & Sunday - May 29th, 30th & 31st, 1987

*I*t was 6:30 am when I awoke to a bright sunny day. The *Sherry D* was riding nicely tied to the dock. I'm glad I prepared my screens yesterday, as the mosquitoes and no-see'ums were terrible. As soon as I put the light on last night, they swarmed the boat. Thank goodness for the "Skin So Soft". I never would have made it through the night without it. I got dressed and took a walk on the beach. It was apparent that the winter had taken its toll. I had remembered this beach as a wide, beautiful expanse; now, even at low tide, the breakers were coming right up to the dunes. The inlet had broken through, and most of the cedar trees were uprooted and blown over.

I know Cedar Island well, as my sister-in-law and her husband had bought land there some years ago and all of us were concerned about the preservation of the island and its fight against the elements. Hopefully, it will remain as one of the prominent barriers in protection of the mainland from the turbulent sea. It is a beautiful island with broad sandy beaches and low lying dunes sometimes covered with cedar and marshes behind — a real sanctuary for birds and wildlife. This seven-mile stretch of sand, about one-half to one mile wide, is cut on the north by the Metompkin Inlet and to the south by the Wachapreague Inlet. Cedar Island is watched carefully by landowners and local people who are concerned about intruders such as myself, and particularly those who may willfully do damage to the island. The environmentalists also take an active role.

It was after I had walked several miles south from the north end of the island, surveying the storm damage that had taken a large part of the beach and dunes over the winter, that I was approached by a group of local workmen who were making their way to a site. To them, I was a stranger and not to be treated with congenial hospitality. They wanted to know who I was, how I got there, what I was doing and what right did I have doing it. Naturally, they didn't believe a word I said. As a matter of fact, at one point I thought I was to be thrown into the ocean to fend for myself.

I learned that their leader was a friend of my sister-in-law who had told me to look him up when I arrived in Wachapreague. He could help me with directions and any assistance I needed while in the area. Well, the assistance that this leader and his men were about to give me was the type I was not really looking for, as that was a quick way off the island. When I explained who I was, my trip, and my relationship to my wife's sister, their attitude changed and they became very friendly. In fact, when they learned how I got there and a little of my voyage, it was suggested that I tie up to their barge in Wachapreague so that my boat could

Beach erosion on Cedar Island after 1986-87 winter storm.

One of the luxurious homes that survived.

I took my bearings here.

ride up and down with the tide. They turned out to be a great help then and later. I probably would never have met them had it not been for my intrusion on the island.

Time and tide are the crucial elements for Cedar Island, one of the most beautiful, famous, and the fastest-eroding of the 14 islands that make up Virginia's 40-mile-long barrier island chain. According to University of Virginia scientists studying barrier islands, the eastern half of the continent is sinking. The barrier islands are moving west to join the mainland, and the Eastern Shore is just a heap of dirt sitting on top of a big rock.

How long these island chains will last is anyone's guess. After the previous winter's storm and the ocean waves beat through Metompkin Inlet, it looked as if Cedar Island would not last. This has happened before, however, but the beach filled in again in time. Nature has a peculiar way of handling these matters and in effect what she takes away, she gives back in another act. This was happening here; where the north end was a wash out, the south end was building up.

In 1962, a powerful March storm virtually swept the island clean, but it had rebuilt itself to the beautiful land mass I had seen just the year before. I was told of one man who paid a North Carolina company $6,000 to shore up his Cedar Island vacation home with sandbags to protect it over the winter. Four months later, the house was gone and his four to five-acre lot is now about the size of a postage stamp, or so he says. As I walked this now-eroded beach, I believed it.

Though there is some development on the island, it is still very sparse. On the north end of the island where most of the damage occurred, some very large and beautiful summer vacation homes have been built. None of these were lost over the winter, but the mean water line (MWL) is getting closer. Of the eight new homes that have been built there, five are planned to move back from the encroaching surf or to the south end of the island. One owner has had his luxurious home moved twice to safer ground.

The lure of Cedar Island is, of course, the opportunity to own a unique front-porch view of what remains an unspoiled sliver of sand surrounded by water. Privacy is supreme and one must venture there by private boat. Tranquillity ranks high on the list. Walking along the beachfront is a step back in time. This is one of the few barrier islands along the East Coast of the United States that is not severely impacted by pollution or development.

It is a haven for bird-watchers, and an area as close to a wild and natural state as you can find on the Atlantic Coast. Your shoes crunch on layers of shells, clams, mussels, oysters and even conch anywhere you walk on the island. University of Virginia scientists are studying this area now with teams of microbiologists from the Department of Environmental Science. They state, "It is one of the very few natural systems left. Finding out how this system operates may, first of all, help us to keep this one intact, and second, enhance another system's quality of life for marine species."

The man who lost his vacation home to the sea that winter, said, "I would do it all again if I had the money. I don't regret my loss for a second. The ocean took it away, but the memories will last forever."

Well, it was time to leave. The sun was high in the sky and I had survived my adventure with the workmen and learned to appreciate their protection of this serene paradise. Making my way back along the beach those few miles to the *Sherry D*, and enjoying the fresh breezes from the ocean, I was looking forward to that sail through the marshes and into Burtons Bay and on to Wachapreague.

It is now 11 am, the tide is flood max and I am heading for Wachapreague. At the rate I'm going, I should be there in no time. I passed several fisherman who didn't appear to be having too much luck. We just passed marker 101 in Cedar Island Bay and I was heading straight for my next green marker when I hit bottom. The wide water was on my right, and I was fairly close on the green marker's line. I pulled in on the sail to heel over, hoping to skim right over; but instead, I dug right into the mud. I tried everything, but to no avail, she just would not budge. It was not quite noontime, and the tide was not expected to change until 4 pm.

After ignoring my predicament for awhile, the men who were fishing finally came over to me. I asked them if they would pull me off and after throwing them a line, they reluctantly gave a half-hearted try (with their motor only at half-throttle) and threw my line back saying "the tide will come in sometime." What a difference between the "good ole boys" I met yesterday, who couldn't do enough, and these guys. I've been stuck here for 2½ hours now. How frustrating! The *Sherry D* is lying way over on her side in about one foot of water, and I can see the drop off about an oar's length away. The wind has stopped; it is 92 degrees, and I'm baking in the sun. The flies are licking the "Skin So Soft" and the no-see'ums are all around, but have not yet attacked. There is nothing to do but try to stay calm, cool and collected and wait for the tide to change which should be about 5 pm. I put up my Bimini to ward off the sun, it works great. I still have plenty of time, Sherry is not expecting me in Wachapreague until 7or 8 pm tonight.

At 5 pm I noticed the tide starting to change and by 6:30 pm the *Sherry D* was almost righted but not quite free. At 7:30 pm we were finally free (that sure was a long 7½ hours). It felt great to be on a level deck again and I motored out of Cedar Island Bay and into Burton's Bay.

It was a beautiful evening, but the sun was going down fast. We were bucking the current, and I had at least 4 miles to go with only one hour of daylight left. I knew I had to stay right on these markers, and with the beautiful southwest wind blowing, I decided to put up the main to help on the speed. With the sail up, I could pick up another 1 to 2 knots and hopefully get into Wachapreague before dark.

I passed marker #14 which had a big osprey roosting in its nest and with the setting sun in the background I couldn't pass up this picture. Just as I tried to snap the shutter, the osprey took off but my camera didn't. Unfortunately, I had it on lock. I chanced turning around in the narrow channel as I had to have this picture. I waited 15 minutes for the bird to return and, when he did, I got my much wanted picture. I came out of Burton's Bay, moving nicely. It was getting dark now, the flashing lights on the markers came on and I mistook #10 for #122, which is not uncommon in the dark, and — Wham! I was on the ground again. I reversed the motor and tried to back off, no luck. I motioned to an oncoming boat to help, but he just waved and kept going. (What happened to that unwritten law of helping people on the water?) I was so angry that I jumped to the stern of the boat, cranked on the motor in its reverse position, put it on full speed, ran up to the mast step and flung my weight out to the side, hanging onto the upper shrouds to heel the boat over as far as I could. I was determined that I was not going to spend the night in this mosquito-plagued marsh. Slowly the *Sherry D* began to back off, and I was once again free. It was now 9 pm as I entered the Wachapreague cut at "122" and made the turn. Now, with the motor only, the current was pushing with me for the first time. I flew in, past the Island House Restaurant where Sherry was waving to me from its deck. I tied up to the barge and quickly put things in order.

Sherry said she could see my masthead light coming across the marsh and, seeing no other sailboats for miles, knew it was me. She had overheard people in the restaurant talking about me and remarking that "he sure had guts." Little did they know that I had no choice and that it would have taken more guts to stay out in that marsh all night. At last I was in Wachapreague.

It is time for rest, play and maintenance. Sherry and I spent the day, Saturday, cleaning the boat, charging batteries, doing laundry and repairing the broken boom prop and the tiller and also managed to get in a little shopping. Sherry's sister and her husband were expected to meet us there later in the afternoon.

Their neighbor in Wachapreague, Doug Douglas, was a great machinist and had a lot of tools. I had been sailing with a broken tiller since the Delaware, and my hands were rough and sore. Now, with Doug's help, we were able to piece it back together securing the two pieces with a six-inch-long lag screw. It worked just fine, looked like new and was stronger than ever.

I had promised to call Robert de Gast when I arrived at Wachapreague. He lived on the same latitude as Wachapreague on Pungoteague Creek, but on the Bay side about 10 miles across as the crow flies. He invited us to see his new house, meet his wife and have cocktails on Sunday night. It was a real treat. Robert is a real gentleman, an interesting person; and his house, which he restored himself, was beautiful. Robert and his wife, Evelyn, made us feel right at home. Upon our leaving, Robert invited me to stop by on my way up the Chesapeake. This I will definitely try to do, as I am sure we can swap adventure stories. It should take me 3 to 4 days to sail from Wachapreague to Pungoteague Creek via Cape Charles, yet only 20 minutes to drive over land that 10 miles. It is late Sunday night and Sherry must return home to Pasadena and I must return to Wachapreague. Tomorrow, I will start my final leg to Oyster, the Magothy Bay and Cape Charles; then up the Chesapeake.

Chapter 14

Day Fifteen & Sixteen Wachapreague to Oyster

Monday & Tuesday - June 1st & 2nd, 1987

I was up and getting ready early. The *Sherry D* was still docked at my friend's barge. I loaded supplies and reinstalled my newly repaired tiller and boom crutch. A Coast Guard boat, returning from Parramore Island, came by and I inquired about tides and dredging information. They recommended that I stick to the VIP (Virginia Inside Passage) except for continuing out to the Quinby Inlet and then back in and joining up with the VIP at marker "176", thereby avoiding a two-foot shoaling area at the lower part of Sloop Channel. I followed their suggestions and had no trouble.

Started out with motor at 11 am, two hours before mean high tide. When I rounded marker "138" at Millstone Creek, a nice breeze came up out of the southeast and I raised the main. I didn't use the headsail as I did not want to block my forward view. The Coast Guard insisted that I stay right in the channel and keep the motor running at slow speed. This worked great. When I reached the Great Machipongo Channel, the breeze was better; but now I had to tack. (When you look at the charts, it appears as if you are surrounded by deep water on each side of the

Sometimes the VIP is very well marked.

Sometimes you can't see land, yet you can have only one to two feet of water below your keel. Where's the channel???

The Log of the Sherry D

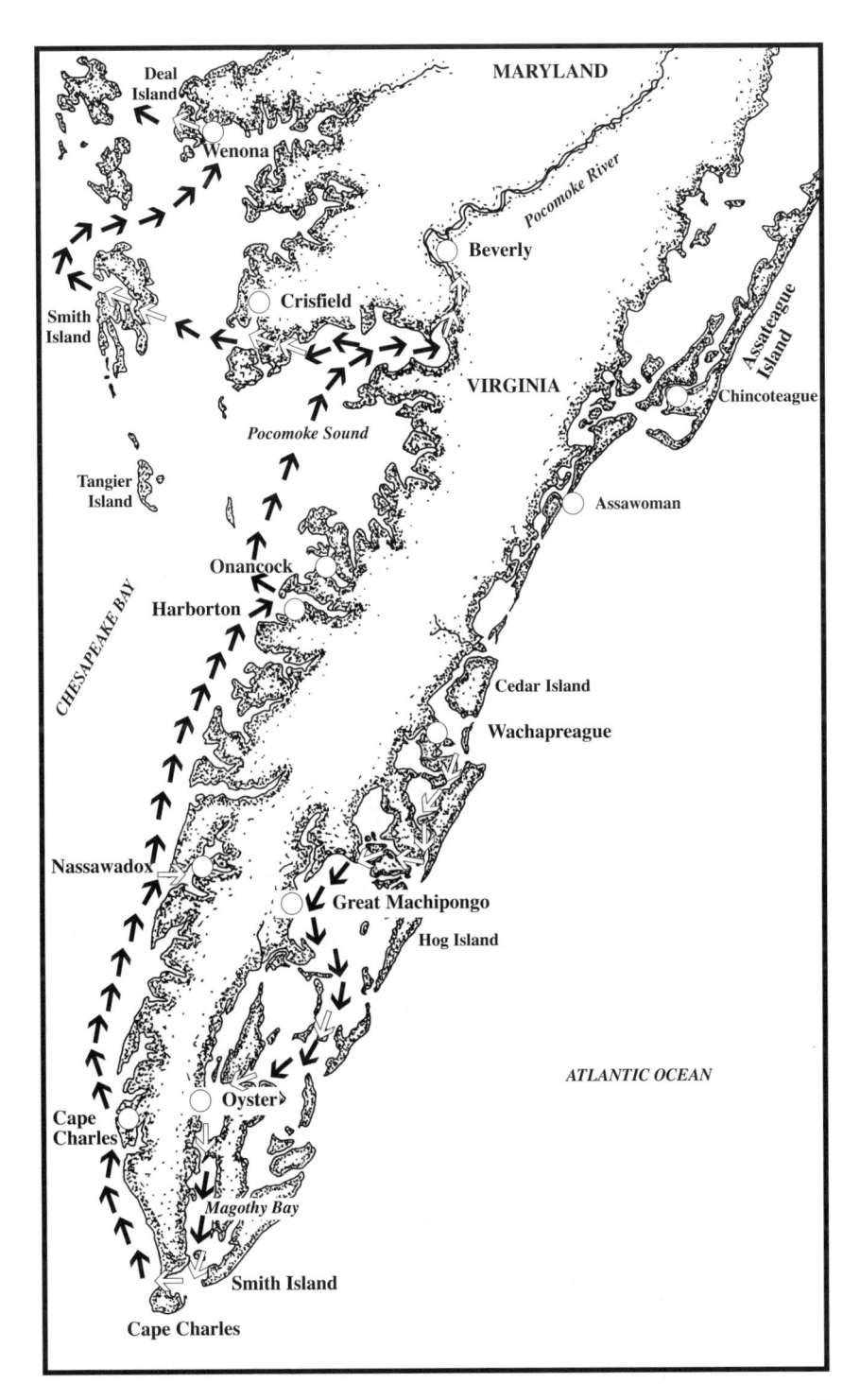

channel; but, in actuality, it is the mud flats and, at high tide, they are two feet under water.) For example, according to the charts there was 30 to 45 feet of water in the middle of the channel, but, once outside of it, there was only two to three feet; yet I couldn't see from one side of Hog Island Bay to the other. What a disappointment, as I had understood that Hog Island was one of the most beautiful islands and I wasn't close enough to see anything. I knew I had better concentrate on this leg of the trip.

Once in the Machipongo Channel, I raised my genoa and was really moving. The wind was blowing hard and the chop was terrific. I clocked it once at 25 miles an hour. That's not too bad for this old lady, but the chop was something else, and so was tacking, not knowing if I was in or out of the channel. Sure enough at marker "194" we hit bottom. I was supposed to be in 45 feet, but a quick glance at my chart indicated four feet and it was low tide. I couldn't understand this as I was on the correct side of red "194". I raised my centerboard, which was down one foot, and was immediately off. I now made my turn and thought I was heading for marker "8" of the Great Machipongo Inlet, but instead I actually saw "196" and "198" on the VIP. I had cut right across uncharted water and didn't know it. The mistake was to my advantage as it had shortened my trip by a good mile.

I called the Coast Guard on my radio and asked for an update on the tides and weather and gave them my position. They said I was doing great but cautioned me to be careful in the stretch between markers "203" and "217" because I would be going through there at mean low and it was only two and a half feet. If I hit, just sit tight and wait for the tide to rise which would be at 10:15 tonight. Sure enough, at marker "214" I was right in the mud, good and tight. It was 5:45 pm and I was ready for a break anyway. I dropped the sails and threw the anchor over. I turned on my marine radio to NOOA Channel #1 and heard a severe weather warning for my area until 8:30 tonight.

No sooner had the warning been broadcast than the sky turned black to the south and the wind began to blow hard. The report called for 40 mph winds with thunderstorms and hail. The wind was hitting us broadside and I knew I had to get the *Sherry D* off the bottom so she could head into the wind. After much hard work and, fortunately a rising tide, she was off. I ran out about 120 feet of anchor line. I wasn't sure which side of the channel I would end up on, but that was the least of my worries. I had to get her bow into the wind and the waves. I clocked the wind at 30 mph. I decided since I was dug in I would spend the night right there and regroup in the morning. It was getting dark and here I was out in the channel in the middle of nowhere. I lit and hung the anchor light in the rigging and went below to celebrate my efforts with a Bloody Mary and some dinner. It started to rain, with thunder and lightning. Nothing left to do but hit the sack. I could hardly keep my eyes open.

Let it rain, let it rain.

We made it through the evening with no problems, until I was rudely awakened at 11:30 pm by the sounds of thunder and the flash of lightning. The wind, whistling through the rigging, sounded like a freight train coming right down the channel. The waves were breaking all around us and the *Sherry D* would raise up, wiggle a little and settle down waiting for the next one as she creaked, grunted and groaned. It was black as pitch outside and, when the lightning would strike, I could see white caps on the water. I was thankful that I had gotten off the bottom and had a long anchor rode. It was now high tide and I was at least two to four feet off the bottom. I was also glad that the *Sherry D*'s bow was pointing into the wind, as the wind would surely have set her over on her side if it hit us broadside. I awoke periodically throughout the night and was reassured that the anchor was holding fast.

I was up at 6:30 am, got dressed and had breakfast. It was low tide again. I went up on deck and saw a commercial fisherman checking his crab pots. He came over to me, offered his "good mornings", and inquired how I was. I told him fine, until last night. He then informed me that I was in the wrong place. The deeper water was next to a little island near by or on the other side of the channel. I told him I was following the channel markers. He looked at me a little funny, then said "thems don't work no mo." He pointed out a new route, which I intend to follow today. Come to find out, I was only 100 yards from being through this shallow channel when I hit. Thank goodness I stopped where I did or else I would have had to anchor in 25-50 feet of water.

It was now 9:30 am and time to pull up the

I spent the night aground here.

"Thems don't work no mo'."

"Follow my wake."

This boat saw too many oyster bottoms.

A clam dredge boat leaving Oyster.

anchor. I have decided to bypass Oyster and go right into the Magothy Bay, probably around Cape Charles and start my way up the Chesapeake. It is a beautiful day, with westerly winds, but a threat of thunderstorms for tonight. I will look for a safe harbor early today.

Taking the old fisherman's advice, instead of following the channel markers, I went out of Spidercrab Bay on the outside of Eckichy Channel and rounded R FL 224 into Sand Shoal Channel. The wind was really blowing hard out of the West, about 15 knots and the chop was something else. I needed the extra head sail because I was bucking the current and the wind. I donned my safety harness, and up I went. I had the working jib up in no time and was moving out. There were several interesting old trawlers and dredge boats coming out of Oyster, so out came my camera. I could see the town of Oyster in the not too far distance and decided to do some sightseeing as it was only 11:30 am.

By noon I was tying up to an old oyster boat next to U.W. West's dock. I had to justify my tying up there so I purchased two gallons of gas. When I went to the grocery to pay for the gas, I bumped into a group of old timers. There were three or four of them all sitting around a big pot-belly stove discussing world affairs while nipping long neck bottles of R.C. Cola. The stove was not lit, but it appeared that this was the town's focal point on a cold day. All that was missing at the time was a cracker barrel and a checker board. Most of the talk was about weather. My ears strained while I was paying for my gas. When I bought a Moon Pie and bottle of R.C., I was accepted into the club. I asked a lot of questions about the route south to Cape Charles. The consensus was that I should have no trouble reaching Cape Charles before dark. However, one said that if I ran into those predicted thunderstorms, I should take shelter inside the old cement ship jetty. One of the old timers, who used to run the Kiptopeake ferry, said that there was plenty of depth on each side of the channel out of Oyster and not to worry.

I thanked them and left to do some sightseeing. Oyster is a small and isolated place and it did not take long. So, with camera in hand, I did the town. Aside from the post office, I found the W.L. Bell Clam Factory to be the most interesting. This is where the large clam dredge boats come in with their catch. The dredges unload their clams into cages for forklifts to pick up from the dock and transport them inside the factory where they are well washed, the clams shucked and then, whatever. A conveyor belt carried out the empty shells and loaded them onto trucks. Where they went from there, I do not know, but I had heard that most of the clams went to Howard Johnson's.

I found this to be another great experience. I had originally planned to bypass Oyster, but I didn't. That's what is so good about a voyage like this. Just do whatever comes along. I was glad that I stopped in Oyster.

I left about 2 pm and no sooner had I rounded R "6", just outside of Oyster heading for G "5", we hit bottom. I was on the outside of G "5" and should have been inside. Instead of following the normal navigational markers I considered the old timer's statement that I had plenty of water all the way. Apparently, they didn't know that I had a sailboat. I was tacking and thought that I had plenty of water (it was high tide) but, no matter what I tried, I still couldn't get off. I was in the mud and the wind was blowing hard right on my nose. I couldn't for the life of me get her to come around to port so I could heel over and lessen my draft. I was only just touching, but my keel would not pivot. Once again, not one of the 30 or so fishing boats that passed me offered to help. They obviously couldn't take the time to help a sailor, not even a wave this time, when they were only interested in their fast boats and their fishing (sure wish those "Good Ole Boys" were here now).

One incoming sport fisherman did offer a hand, but once he couldn't pull me off he took my anchor out to deeper water for me (so I could pull myself to deeper water when the tide came in.) I was in sight of Oyster all this

Above: W.L. Bell & Son clam factory.

Left: U.S. Post Office, Oyster, Virginia.

time and I'm sure the old timers had a good laugh as they looked across the channel at this crazy sailor, laid over on their oyster shell bottom.

It is now 8 pm and the *Sherry D* is still sitting high and dry. The next high tide isn't for three or four hours. May as well use this time for some maintenance work. I had pulled my starboard winch out when pulling in the anchor earlier to try and winch myself off, so I repaired that, changed oil in the lower unit of the outboard and worked on the gears (I had no neutral). It had been a hot and frustrating day. After the maintenance was complete, I sat back and relaxed with a few beers. The no-see'ums have arrived and are starting to bite. As discouraging as the events of today were, there is a real beauty and tranquillity in the marsh. There is a lot to see, with the birds hovering overhead, the many boats going in and out of the channel and the oysters which I can see now growing right under my hull. The sun is setting and I have soft music playing on the radio. May as well accept this predicament as good therapy, and, what the heck, I'll just be a day later getting to Cape Charles. It is a small price to pay.

High tide came in about 11:45 pm and I moved off just scraping bottom, heading by motor through the channel into the open waters in line with the VIP again. At 1 am, I was once again anchored and ready for bed. My plan is to start out early in the morning with a low tide and start through the VIP when tide is low and hope to slide down the Magothy Bay with the flood tide.

I was aground here from 2:30 pm until 11:30 pm.

Thirty boats must have passed me and only one stopped to help.

CHAPTER 15

Day Seventeen & Eighteen – Oyster to Cape Charles and Pungoteague Creek

Wednesday & Thursday - June 3rd & 4th, 1987

I awoke again to a beautiful morning. Radio weather indicated hazy but clearing, hot and sunny with alternating clouds and a threat of thunderstorms this afternoon. After a quick breakfast, I'm ready to raise sails, up anchor and start down the Mockhorn Channel which starts at marker G"233". The chart indicates 23 to 39 feet all the way south until I hit the Magothy Bay when I once again go through a narrow stretch. We'll worry about that later.

By 8 am, there was a four to five-knot southeast wind and the tide is starting to rise. An hour later I passed "248" and entered Magothy Bay. The weather has taken a drastic change. Heavy haze has set in; it is almost like a fog. The humidity is 85 percent, and it looks as if it will rain any minute; but there's still a nice southeast breeze and I'm making good time. I am running with the current with only the main up. The temperature has dropped fast, it is now 62 degrees. The radio station, Channel 93 out of Norfolk, is still calling for bright skies, with temperatures in the 90s. Norfolk is only 30 miles south of here; this is crazy! If all goes well, I should be going under the Cape Charles Bridge/Tunnel around lunchtime.

I have just passed marker "255", I'm through the cut and again in good water according to my charts. I scraped bottom one time in the middle of the channel and wondered how those big trawlers come through from Cape Charles to Oyster. I'm taking one marker at a time. It is a strange experience, as I can only see one marker at a time. Just when I think I'm going to run out and nearing one marker, the next one comes into sight. I am constantly checking my compass for the heading to that next marker just in case the fog socks in. This portion of the trip has a charm of its own. Occasionally I will see a land mass and then it disappears.

I just passed very close to marker "261". The chart says I am in 27 feet, but I felt something and threw the leadline over. I was in only four feet of water. Now comes the fun at my next marker, R "262". I must turn southwest into the very tight Cape Charles Channel. (We made it through without a hitch.)

Shortly before noon, we went under the bridge; we were now in the Chesapeake. By later afternoon I was anchored in Nassawadox Creek, a beautiful little sheltered area with nice houses around it (this is more like the anchorage I'm used to, with its nice coves, high banks and calm waters). Even a few nice sailboats and yachts were tied to private docks. Some young people in a Boston Whaler came by me water skiing. They waved and called a welcome. This was the Bay-side; a whole different atmosphere.

What a sail up the Chesapeake! We went 26 miles straight up on a broad reach with winds southeast 16 to 20 knots. That's clocking five and a half knots average, give or take one-half hour anchoring and motoring. I passed the cement ships' breakwater at the old Kiptopeake ferry site. This was the place the old-timers told me was a good and safe harbor, but they failed to mention all the fish nets blocking the entrance they told me to use. It must have been great fishing there, as it took me one-half hour dodging sport fishermen (it was drum fishing season). The rest of the way was easy. I just followed and dodged the crab pots the other 24 miles. I really didn't mind though, as I was moving fast, it was fun and kept me on my toes.

I hated to quit sailing so early in the day, I still had four hours of daylight left, but the radio station at Hampton Roads was giving tornado warnings and possible thunderstorms with high winds and hail until 9 pm. We had journeyed 40 miles today (the most I had ever done in one day on this trip) and I was tired. Time to update my log and fix myself a Bloody Mary. I also didn't want to press my luck. I decided it was a good time to refill my gas tank from the spare one on the foredeck and, as luck would have it, I accidentally knocked my good and faithful hat overboard and the breeze took it just out of my reach. That hat was very special to me as it was the one that went overboard in the Delaware and came swimming back to me. It was a special part of this boat and this trip. I upped anchor and started the motor to try and get it, but, no use, it sank and was gone forever. My heart ached and I grieved over its loss. I re-anchored and finished filling my gas tank (hatless). The radio blasted a tornado watch from Hampton Roads to Baltimore. A twister had already touched down in southern Virginia on the other side of the Bay. I hoped and prayed it would pass us by. I fell asleep reading some more of *The Sot-Weed Factor*.

Just out of reach.

DAY 18

Thursday - June 4, 1987

At 7 am I was up and dressed. There was a little thunder, lightning and rain last night but nothing to worry about. Supplies are running out. I must stock up soon. Also, I have run out of water and ice (maybe Robert de Gast can help me get supplies along with the offer of a hot shower). In my Army days, I learned to bathe, brush my teeth and have a drink (not necessarily in that order) with just a canteen cup of water. Could I manage to do that?

It is a cloudy and muggy morning with no wind. I get out my charts and study them while having a cup of coffee and a slice of bread. I will motor the two miles into the Bay. Once there, I turn right at the green and red traffic light (navigational markers), and head for Pungoteague Creek which is 16 miles north. It is 9:05 am and I'm writing in my log when I spot a little yellow airplane out at the mouth of the river doing flip flops. I wonder if Robert, who has his own plane, is looking for me — I'm ready to up anchor.

What a difference. I feel like I'm back in home territory again. People are waving and it is peaceful with its high banks and trees. The Channel was the easiest to follow that I have seen in a long time. All I did was follow the crab pots on each side of me, as I went out. It was like the fishermen had paved a road for me. They followed in the same line as the red and green buoys, except at times they varied a little. I elected to follow the crab pot trail and went right out. As I passed the entrance marker to Nassawadox Creek R"2", the Bay was covered with a heavy haze and there was very little visibility. I took a few readings on my chart and judged I was doing about four knots with motor only. (I had broken my portable knot meter in some rough weather back on the Metompkin Bay, before Cedar Island.)

I decided to run on 320 degrees for four to five miles. I should be about one-half mile from BW at "2c" then set a course on 33 degrees and stay on it until noon. I was hoping the haze would lift by then but, if not, I would continue on with compass in hand. I looked up and saw a large black object off in the haze. I thought this bay was really marked well. I wondered why I had not seen that yesterday when I was coming in.

It didn't take me long to realize that I was looking at a large freighter coming down the Bay. It was the largest ship I had seen since leaving Delaware Bay some 10 days ago. Then, when I was looking for the channel marker, I spotted a large school of porpoises. They were popping up all over but too far out of range for a picture. I turned on the motor hoping to pique their curiosity, but they stayed off in the distance, just playing with me. When I was too far off, they would jump up out of the water with bodies arched in a beautiful progression; then, as I closed in, they would disappear only to come up again a hundred or so yards on the other side of me. I spent about one-half hour circling in order to get some pictures, then decided it was time to get back on a 33 degree course. What else will this day bring?

The seas are perfect for trolling, so I decided to rig my bluefish popper and try it out. If I was successful, I could exchange my catch for Robert de Gast's

Harborton Town Dock and its carved phrase.

hospitality. Lord knows I would never be able to clean and prepare one out here. In fact, I sure hope I don't catch too many. My worries were for naught. Oh well, the de Gasts will not be dining on bluefish this night. I had high hopes after hearing Bud Jenkin's tales about the bluefish poppers hitting the water and all the blues rushing to it (I have no doubt, however, that had Bud been here we would have had to abandon ship due to the abundance of fish onboard.)

I followed my course right into Pungoteague Creek. Still no wind even though I kept the main up in wishful anticipation of such. At 3:30 pm I was just rounding the bend to Harborton and caught the wind coming right out of Pungoteague Creek (Robert de Gast had been keeping it all for himself.) It has been hazy and threatening all day, and I am glad I'm a bit ahead of schedule as the sky is turning black with heavy rain clouds overhead.

After tying up at the Harborton Town Dock, I asked a very friendly gentleman (his name was "Parks") where I could buy gas and get some fresh water. He informed me there was no fresh water around and that I could find some gas about a mile up the road. I asked if he knew Robert de Gast and he said "Yes, of course, everyone knows Robert." He pointed out his house and told me it was high tide and I could sail over there. I wasn't thrilled about sailing in on a high tide which meant that I would be on the ground when it went out. I asked if there was a phone I could use, and he said that the phone was at the same place where the gas was (a mile up the road). He offered to call Robert for me from his house as he was going back home which was only a few hundred yards up the road. I went about straightening up the boat. In no time Mr. Parks returned saying that Robert would be right over in his little rubber boat. While I waited for Robert, I walked around the dock to stretch my legs and to see the sights. I couldn't help but notice an interesting epithet carved into boards on the dock:

> *"God Bless the Boys who make the Noise*
> *on the Southside of Pungoteague Creek."*

I thought this to be interesting and I wondered if Mr. Parks had been one of those boys in his youth. As I continued down the dock, I then spied an old row boat with a "Calle" outboard motor on the back. This was an old magneto start motor just like one that my father had when I was a boy. I knew how good the Calle motors were and here was living proof. The old motor and possibly the boat were over 50 years old and still running. Harborton was my kind of town. At least there was reason to believe that there was more to see. It's another one of those places that I made a mental note, "I must return."

Soon, Robert arrived and we exchanged greetings and small talk about the weather and the trip so far. He was somewhat concerned about the cold front coming in and we decided it would be a good idea if I tied up to a mooring piling (in fact, the same one Robert had used for his large boat) because the *Sherry D* could ride out a hurricane there, if one hit. He told me to close up the boat and come home with him for a much needed hot shower and dinner. I was also expected to stay overnight at his house in a nice, soft bed. I was really tired from the sail from Oyster and welcomed all of these suggestions.

After a shower, we had a long talk about my trip thus far, his work and about this part of the country. Robert is very happy with his new life here and I get the impression that he and Evelyn never plan to leave. Evelyn had the duty at her real estate office that night. Morris, Robert's friend, joined us for a cold beer at Hopkins Wharf in Onancock (I had traveled 92 miles in the past 3 days to get there, yet by land it was only 10 miles from where I started in Wachapreague). We had dinner at a little restaurant in Onley Shopping Center, where I had stopped four days earlier for supplies. Again, I was able to stock up on supplies on our way home and filled my gas cans. Robert supplied me with fresh water and ice cubes from his freezer. After another good hot shower and clean clothes that I had taken from their dryer, I was ready for that soft bed and to continue another leg of my journey in the morning.

Robert de Gast came in his little rubber boat.

"I spied an old rowboat with a Calle outboard motor on the back."

CHAPTER 16

Day Nineteen & Twenty-Pungoteague Creek to Pocomoke River

Friday & Saturday - June 5th & 6th, 1987

After a comfortable night in the de Gasts' guest room we had breakfast. Robert transported me in his little rubber boat back to the *Sherry D* where she was riding beautifully at her mooring. I gathered everything together, raised her sails and started out Pungoteague Creek, heading to the Pocomoke; it was 10:30 am.

I had called the "Good Ole Boys" (Van Wilkerson and Jim Dykes) last night and told them I would be making my way to the Pocomoke today and should arrive there sometime late afternoon. I was looking forward to seeing them again.

I was sailing out of Pungoteague Creek on a nice northeasterly and was moving right along until I turned northeast at the mouth of the creek. Onancock was the next creek up the chain and now, not only was the wind on my nose, but the tide was changing and the current was coming right down the Bay. After tacking, I still couldn't make much headway. There was a large grayish black area over the Western Shore, and I could see heavy rain in the direction of the Rappahannock River. I watched a small white cloud forming a spout and prayed it was not a water spout. I was in the widest part of the Bay, moving northeast, and the storm was heading south down the Bay. I was sure this was the cold front coming in, which did not help me one bit. It was time to prepare for some heavy weather again: I took down the main and left the jib in place, and the motor running.

I had one heck of a time finding my markers. It seemed like I was really traveling fast, but I thought I would never cross the mouth of Onancock Creek. Watts Island was visible way off my port bow, and it took forever to get there, as the wind and tide kept pushing me back to the Eastern Shore.

The tide was starting to run into Pocomoke Sound now; and, to make headway, I decided to take my chances and fell off on the reachway far to the southeast of Marker R "8" and cut across the sandbar off Long Point. My chart showed three feet where I would cut across, and my heart was in my mouth. It was an incoming tide and it wasn't that I minded so much going aground (Lord knows I've done that enough on this trip, I'm used to it); but, should I hit, I feared the waves would pound us to death before I could get her off. I followed (and dodged) the line of crab pots and fishing stakes and finally saw a white and black marker and headed for it. As it turned out, it was the marker defining the Maryland/Virginia state line. This brought to mind a passage that I had recently read in *The Sot-Weed Factor*: "A noble ship, from deck to peaks akin to those that Homer's Greeks sail'd east to Troy in days of yore, as we sail'd now to Maryland's Shore."

I crossed back into Maryland at 5:30 pm. I was home again but not yet free. I was a little off course but going in the right direction. My chart indicated that once I passed these markers I would be right into the Pocomoke River narrow channel. Now I was running free, and the wind was pushing me right along. I raised the main and took down the jib as it was flopping from side to side. With the main alone, I was doing five and a half knots. The waves still were very high due to the Sound being so open and shallow. I was drenched and worn out. I reached the narrow cut at Williams Point that brought me to the Pocomoke River and followed the markers and stakes which, at times, brought me within a stone's throw of the shoreline.

At last I rounded and came into the sharp and narrow cut through Williams Point. To my relief, it was slick ca'm water again. I sailed up this desolate but beautiful river with good winds and no waves. The tide was running with me as I rounded the turns through the marshes. I was in heaven again and I couldn't resist playing my Palauan tape as the *Sherry D* carried me through this serene wilderness. It was beautiful, and I was only starting to see the Pocomoke.

Tranquility.

Jim and Van had told me that the big brick house with the dock and white pilings was only about four miles into the river and that they would be looking for me. Sure enough, there it was as they had described. I saw a small red and white airplane sitting in a field in the back of the main house. It was a beautiful place. Not knowing if the owner was home, I sailed 500 yards further up to the "Cedar Hall" boat ramp. There were Jim and Van waiting with all smiles, and they quickly rushed out to grab my line with one hand while holding a cold beer in the other.

I decided to tie up at the ramp and just relax. We had a couple of beers and sat in the cockpit, laughing, and they told me they had been watching me come up the river for the past 30 minutes. They saw only my sail over the marsh, but knew it had to be me. It was 7 pm when I tied up and they had been on the lookout for me since 3:30 pm. They had almost given up when they saw my sail. While sitting there having my beer and watch-

With friends at last, but . . .

ing a beautiful sunset, one of the largest barges I had seen came past, pulled by a very powerful tug called the *Bay Bird*.

We went by car to Van's mother's restaurant, the Eastern Shoreman, just south of Pocomoke City, and had crab cakes. They were good. Jim promised to pick me up the next morning to get gas, water, supplies and then to take me on a motorboat tour of the Pocomoke all the way to Snow Hill. When I arrived back at the boat about 10:30 pm, I jumped into my bunk and slept like a log.

Day 20

Saturday - June 6, 1987

As promised last night, Jim came by in his pickup truck, and we left for Van's chicken farm where Jim kept his boat on a trailer. Van's farm was something else — he raised about 7,500 hens and there was one rooster for every eight or nine hens. Van owned the chicken house and all the equipment; but Perdue owned the chickens and the feed. There they produced hatching eggs for Perdue. Van collected the eggs daily, culled them and then shipped the hatching eggs to another farm for incubation. He collected about 4,000 eggs each day. Jim and I picked up the boat and left Van talking to his chickens. On the way back to launch Jim's boat at Cedar Hall, I bought the supplies I needed. As Jim launched, I checked to make sure the *Sherry D* was secure. Once onboard Jim's boat, we pushed off into the current and tried to start the engine. We could not get it started and drifted downstream. After being towed back into the dock by a passing powerboater, we spent the rest of the day working on the motor at a mechanic's house. Needless to say, I did not get a motorboat tour of the Pocomoke. A real loss, as it is a very scenic river.

I learned a lot about the Pocomoke River, however, and soon realized that it was another of those great finds that I must come back to see some day. There is so much there to see, do and study. If you are in a hurry, just forget it as Corwith Cramer reminds me, by his quotation in the *Chesapeake Skipper*, that "Poking up the Pocomoke" is the

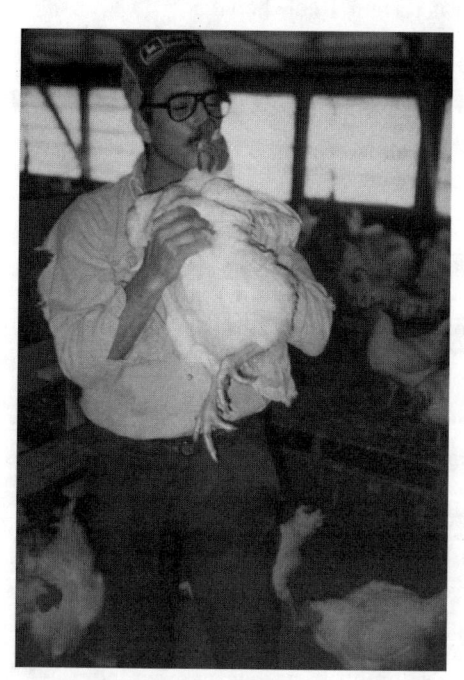

Van and his chickens.

way to do it. One could spend years just poking along. Though I didn't have time to poke, I did have time to listen and I talked to Jim and Van and some of the other locals about the river. Then Jim loaned me several books about the Pocomoke River. One was a nice little pamphlet written in 1966 by one of his relatives, Charles C. Kensey. Mr. Kensey had grown up on the Pocomoke and wrote about that only river in Worcester County, Maryland.

The Pocomoke River rises in the Great Burnt Swamp area in the southern part of Sussex County, Delaware and flows across Worcester County, Maryland. It flows south about thirty miles to Snow Hill, much of which is non-navigable except for a canal. Then it twists and turns southwest another forty miles from Snow Hill to Williams Point and empties into the Pocomoke Sound. The river's entire length is about seventy miles. The name Pocomoke is of Indian origin and means "dark waters." This dark, almost black coloring comes from the many cypress trees and roots that line the shores and swamps.

The navigable part of the river from the Sound to Snow Hill was a major source of boat traffic in the early days and supported commerce between Baltimore and Snow Hill via side-wheeler ships. Steam tugs were often seen towing as many as three two-hundred-foot barges loaded with lumber from North Carolina. Today, diesel tugs tow much larger barges loaded with a good grade of sand to the glass factories at West Point across the Chesapeake and up the York River. The river is noted for its depth. It is said to be the deepest river in the United States for its width. The average depth in the channel is 30 to 40 feet with some places being as deep as 90 feet. Its width is only about 100 yards.

There was all kinds of boat traffic up and down the river. Snow Hill and Pocomoke City were busy shipbuilding towns. Ships, barges and boats of all types were built in great numbers from the war of 1812 to 1920. Then the yards went out of business because there was no longer a demand for wooden ships. Many two-, three- and four-masted ships were at one time built at Pocomoke City yards.

The Atlantic Ocean tides control the flow of water in and out of the Pocomoke. Flood tides flow upstream for five hours at three to four miles per hour. Ebb tide flows down stream at the same rate for seven hours into the Pocomoke Sound which empties into the Chesapeake Bay and then to the Atlantic. The ebb tide carries along a great amount of mud and fine silt which for centuries has been accumulating and forming what is locally known as The Muds. This deposit reaches a mile or so into the Sound making it difficult for large boats to get into the mouth of the river in spite of the river's ample depth. How well I know. The Muds are constantly shifting and dredging, plus replacing of markers, is required.

The river is so interesting and its beauty is unbelievable. Each aspect of its flora and fauna, wildlife, bridges, river traffic, its people and its history could command a chapter each. Not to mention its future. I feel that I have obtained another area of study. I must return.

Jim managed a large dairy farm just outside the Pocomoke called Hollands Farms and on the way back to the boat we stopped there for a tour. Jim was a graduate of the University of Maryland and had majored in Agriculture there.

Again, we had something in common, as I had also attended the University but a few years before Jim. It was now my turn to learn something about dairy farming. The farm had 175 Holstein cows and produced 850 pounds of milk per day. They ship whole milk and it is sold by the pound. Everything was automated. It was quite interesting.

After the tour, we returned to the *Sherry D*. Van was waiting for us and told me the Shettles, the owners of Beverly, were home and wanted to meet me. It wasn't long before William Shettle and his family arrived in their station wagon to carry us back to Beverly. The place was one of the most impressive plantations I have ever seen and the Shettles were lovely people. William Shettle insisted that I move the *Sherry D* to his dock where I would have electricity and security. Then they insisted that I spend the night at the house. We moved the boat and then Van and Jim had to leave. William and I talked long into the night about my trip and my experience going into Cedar Island, on the oceanside. William knew the island well, as he owned a large portion of the north end of the island at Metompkin Inlet that unfortunately had been washed away during the winter storms. Another coincidence, as I had just walked and surveyed that area a week ago.

William's son, Arthur, was very interested in my trip and I lent him my copy of Robert de Gast's book, which he spent most of the night reading. He was most impressed but disappointed that Beverly was not mentioned in the book when Robert talked about the Pocomoke. (Robert de Gast really missed that one, as Beverly is the oldest and finest plantation on the Eastern Shore.) All the Shettles like to sail, especially Arthur, who had just returned from Maine where he sailed and raced off Bar Harbor with his grandfather in their 44-foot Hinkley. I promised them that I would take them for a sail in the *Sherry D* before I left the next day. It would not be like sailing a Hinkley at Bar Harbor, but to sail a 22-foot Sailmaster on the Pocomoke would be an experience. They were all for it.

It was my good fortune to have arrived at Beverly when I did, and to meet Arthur, as he was only visiting his parents for a few days before returning to Chapel Hill, North Carolina, where he was a senior at the University of North Carolina. I could appreciate Arthur's fondness of Beverly and watched the sparkle in his eye as he and his father, William, told me stories of the plantation.

Aside from Sotterly Plantation (1717) on the Patuxent River of the western shore, Beverly (1732) is one of the oldest, still-working plantations in the United States. There have been only two families that have owned it since its original land grant to Donaeck Dennis in 1732, possibly by the Fifth Lord Baltimore, Charles Calvert. William's father, Arthur, and his mother, Emily, bought Beverly from Judge Samuel Dennis of Baltimore in 1936. I read a letter dated November 12, 1936, written to Mr. & Mrs. Arthur Shettle from Samuel K. Dennis, Chief Judge of the Supreme Bench of Baltimore City. This was a letter congratulating the Shettles on their recent purchase of Beverly. Judge Dennis went on to state that, "I, as well as my father, grandfather, brothers and sisters, were all born at Beverly. I always had golden memories and sincere pride in and affection for the place." It must have been difficult for Judge Dennis to sell this grand estate that had remained in his family for more than 200 years.

The original land grant in 1732 to Judge Dennis' great-grandfather was 1500 acres. It was probably Donaeck Dennis, but some say it was his son, who built the main house about 1764. The stone foundation which still supports the original hand-cut beams were probably all locally procured. The walls are built with red brick of the finest clay. They are still magnificently cemented true. The size of the brick and the rich reddish color indicates that they were probably brought over from England, perhaps paid for with tobacco grown at Beverly.

The Shettles: Arthur, William, Renee, their three Labs, and ???

Much history lies within these brick walls. Some of it is known and documented and some is only surmised. I have a feeling that there is much yet unknown, as those beautiful heart-pine paneled woodwork walls inside don't tell the whole story, neither do the ancient trees and well-groomed shrubbery, nor the headstones in the family graveyard.

Apparently, Judge Dennis did try to retain the plantation but, after years of prosperity, the Dennis' fortune was lost during the Great Depression of '29. Most of the 1500 acres were sold off to meet expenses and to maintain other assets. Finally in 1936, when the estate had dwindled to the house and 15 acres, William's father and mother were able to purchase the property from the saddened judge.

It was Beverly's good fortune now, and the senior Arthur and Emily Shettle were able to claim ownership in good stead and had the means to restore and reclaim most of the original site. Today, 900 of the original 1500 acres have been brought back. Most of the farm, along with the house, has been restored to its original condition.

The property was not obtained without conditions, however. One of the interesting contingencies, I thought, was that Uncle Richard be allowed to live out his life at Beverly and to be provided burial with his people in the slave cemetery located on the property. Uncle Richard was born a slave at Beverly and was seven years old when Abraham Lincoln was assassinated on April 14, 1865. He died at Beverly in 1965 at the age of 107. The Shettles honored their commitment to Judge Dennis, and Uncle Richard lies at rest on the property where he was born.

When the Shettles took possession of the property in 1936, they found Uncle Richard still living in one portion of the servants' quarters in an upstairs room,

The main house at Beverly.

where he also kept his chickens that ran free through the house. He was the last of the old help remaining and he cared for the property as best he could. Judge Dennis and all other members of the family had long before moved to Baltimore and elsewhere.

The senior Shettles, realizing that there was much to learn about Beverly and its history, had the foresight to have Uncle Richard record his experiences at Beverly on tape. I did not hear the tape, but William and Arthur told me stories of how Uncle Richard had remembered Union troops riding through Beverly on their regular patrols. They stopped to rest and water their horses there.

Later, as Master Samuel Dennis became a judge, Uncle Richard became his coachman and drove him by horse and carriage to Baltimore and back many times. The trip would take three days one way, and they had certain stops they would make along the way.

Uncle Richard must have been a likable and faithful employee. William told me that he always spoke kindly about his employers and how well he was taken care of. As William was growing up, and later his son Arthur, they got to know and appreciate him.

Another interesting and pleasing feature that I learned about is the delicate, wrought-iron archway over the stone steps of the main house facing the riverside, which contains a lantern to guide mariners up the crooked river at night. It is said that, during the Civil War, Beverly was used as a way station for the underground railway to hide runaway slaves from the South on their way to Pennsylvania and freedom. The lantern had a dual purpose: when lit it was a signal that all was well and safe to come in. The slaves would be hidden in the cellar during the day and then travel farther up the river the next night, probably to Pocomoke City or to Snow Hill, where other cellar houses were located. The archway that held the lantern was supported by a pair of odd wrought-iron creatures that are usually described as ducks, but it can be seen if you look closely that they are intended to be coiled serpents. Ducks don't have forked tongues!

Though Beverly was a slave-holding plantation, the main house and most living quarters lay north of the Maryland line. The farming area reached south into Virginia. Maryland, being a border state, was divided in its sympathies. Beverly was further divided, as Virginia elected to leave the Union and joined the Confederacy. Maryland on the other hand stayed with the Union. Apparently, Uncle Richard's parents had a choice to stay on at Beverly or not. It appeared that they stayed, but no longer as slaves, for Uncle Richard remained there for 100 years after the Civil War.

Some changes did take place in the design of the homestead after the Shettles' purchase. The main house, a large, three-story brick mansion, was separated from the servants' quarters, which consisted of a much smaller, two-story wooden clapboard structure with a brick floor kitchen. The kitchen had a very large, walk-in fireplace for cooking and heating. Of course each room in the main house had its own fireplace. The second story, which housed the servants, consisted of low-ceilinged rooms, each about 10 feet by 10 feet with its own small fireplace. These two buildings were connected by a breezeway which allowed the servants to carry meals from the kitchen to the main house's spacious dining room without regard to weather.

One of Mrs. Shettle's first architectural decisions was to enclose the breezeway and make a nice modern kitchen with an adjoining breakfast room that looked out over the spacious lawns and to the river. The old brick floor kitchen with the walk-in fireplace became a study for Mr. Shettle. The upstairs servants' quarters were retained in their original style with the low ceilings, but the clapboard inner walls were insulated and stuccoed over. The fireplaces remained, along with the wide board floors. The chickens, and possibly Uncle Richard, were moved. The rooms were nicely furnished in the old English style and now became lovely guest rooms. Needless to say, a modern guest bathroom was also centrally built on the

The archway holding the lantern at the entrance overlooking the river.

The Gun Room at Beverly.

The large fireplace in the Gun Room.

second floor. The old, original steps, with deep grooves well worn into their treads from years of use, were finished off, but left in place.

The Shettles were New Yorkers and during World War II contributed their services to the war effort by opening the Beverly mansion to entertain many high ranking military personnel and civilians from Philadelphia, Norfolk, and Washington. The guest rooms were well used, and they showed me letters of appreciation and photos autographed by many of the dignitaries who slept there. One source I read since my return indicates that "George Washington, [Benjamin] Franklin, and the owner himself had congregated there and discussed the embryonic cradle of liberty — a first conception of a United States." I saw no autographed photos of this meeting, but I could realize its possibility.

William and Renee insisted that I be their guest and stay overnight at the house, rather than on the *Sherry D*. When they learned that I had been a Lieutenant Colonel in the U.S. Army, they laughed and said that I qualified. I would sleep in one of the upstairs guest rooms. I was honored, as many notables had slept there, and so did Uncle Richard and now myself.

The favorite room of the main house now appears to be the old brick floor kitchen that was made into a study for Mr. Shettle. It is referred to as the Gun Room. It is furnished with old English wooden tables and chairs. A large brown leather couch sits along one wall and a heavy leather arm chair sits next to it. The walk-in fireplace is the focus of the room. A large wild turkey, mounted with wings spread, hangs from the ceiling. The walls and ceiling with its hand-hewn wooden beams, are hung with every conceivable mounted trophy of wild bird, deer, fish,

lanterns and model ships. On one wall hangs an authentic punt gun, perhaps this is where the "gun" room obtained its name. There is an inscription that reads:
> "The last of its kind used"
> MARKET OR PUNT GUN
> Length: 7 ft. 6 in., wt. 66 lbs.
> Load: 1 lb. Black Powder
>   2 lbs. Shot
> Bore: 2 in.
> Guns greatest kill: 107 Redheads (Redheads are a species of duck)
> From Tangier, Virginia.

William told me that these were all old trophies of his father's, who had retired from being a New York stock broker when he bought Beverly in 1936. He loved it there, as did William's mother, Emily. William's father, Arthur, died in 1961 and his mother in 1975. From her photographs and words from William, Emily Shettle must have been a beautiful and fashionable lady, one who fit well within the decor of Beverly.

William and Renee, along with their lovely little daughters, Natalie and Caroline, made Beverly their permanent residence in 1988, after commuting from Philadelphia on weekends for 10 years. William's son Arthur, and sister Ann, children from a first marriage, try to visit as often as they can. All contribute to the welfare of Beverly, as did the senior Shettles and the Dennises.

There is not much written about Beverly, and I don't know why. Perhaps, because the Dennis family avoided placing it on the National Register of Historical Places. It was their private home and it must have been depressing to see this magnificent estate dwindle in its stature. Now the Shettles have listed Beverly on the National Register of Historic Places and also on the State of Maryland's registry. Although it is not open to the public on a regular basis, the Shettles do open it for tours to the public upon special request and for special occasions.

This has been another real and true experience in my travels. It is one that I probably would have passed up, as did Robert de Gast, had I not met those "Good Ole Boys," Van Wilkerson and Jim Dykes, back on Assawoman Island. Fate plays a mysterious part in our lives. Because of that grounding, I met two good friends, another nice family, recorded an interesting passage in the Log and added another chapter in my life. For this, I feel good.

The plantation was not always called Beverly and I don't know how it came to be called Beverly. It was originally called Thrumcapped. "Thrum" means the end of a weaver's thread. Perhaps Donaeck Dennis felt that this was the end of a long line from his homeland in Ireland. In these more recent days, Beverly is better known as Beverly Manor. After this night, I felt as if I had reached the peak of my trip. I wanted to stay, but I had a journey to finish and a waiting family at home. Tomorrow I must sail for Crisfield.

Chapter 17

Day Twenty-one - Pocomoke River to Crisfield

Sunday - June 7th, 1987

I was up early, before the others, so I dressed quietly, then went outside and walked the grounds. After last night's conversation, I was fascinated. There are 900+ acres which extend from Maryland into Virginia. Needless to say, I did not walk them all. I found the brick-walled private family cemetery and took the liberty of opening the wrought-iron gate and going inside to read the inscriptions on the headstones. Some read as if they came from *Who's Who*, and many dated back to the late 1700s and early 1800s. Then I found the pet cemetery a little farther on and closer to the river, where I found buried many breeds of obviously well-loved dogs, including Labradors, each with a headstone denoting a title.

When I returned, William was up and smiling. He had made a pot of coffee. We had a cup and he then took me on a grand tour of the mansion, inside and out. I could understand his feelings towards the place as he explained many of the details we had talked about last night. He insisted that I sign the guest book that dated back to 1938 and contained the signatures of many notables, the first signature being that of Judge Samuel Dennis. I was extremely honored that my name would also be included here. I signed the register and attempted a short sentence to portray my appreciation for the Shettles' hospitality, but words just could not justify my true feelings in that respect and I prayed that I did not appear to be foolhardy in my writing.

Renee had prepared breakfast by this time and we sat in the breakfast room talking and looking across the river and the marshes when we saw the tug, *Bay Bird*, pulling a barge loaded with piles of sand. Across the marsh, we could see her make her turns around the sharp bends in the river, disappearing only to come into view at the next turn. William told me that he had lost three docks to these barges when they cut too close rounding the turn just north of Beverly. He recommended that I radio the captain of the barge on channel 13 and ask if I should move the sailboat now resting at the end of Beverly's dock. The captain of the *Bay Bird* immediately returned my call, was appreciative of the fact that I was willing to move and suggested that it would be a good idea if I moved on the inside of the dock. He had a 438-foot tow and the current was running pretty heavy. Sometimes when rounding that turn, the current would hit the tow and swing it in towards the dock. It took an unwieldy maneuver to straighten the tow out. It was best not to take any chances. He readily admitted that he had carried that dock away at least once before. After hearing this and having heard William's horror tales, I prepared to move without hesitation. I had plenty of time and just untied the lines and swung her around to the inside of the dock.

Feeling better now, I returned to the house, had another cup of coffee and we watched the *Bay Bird* with her tow pass without incident. After she was clear, I took the Shettles for a short sail in the *Sherry D*. The wind was blowing nicely and we used each of the river bends to change our tacks. On the way back to Beverly, she was again running free, then close hauled and/or on a reach at every turn. It was like being back on the Smyrna River again. The Shettles loved the boat and asked if I knew of any like her for sale. I didn't, but thought that if I wanted, I could have sold the *Sherry D* right then and there. But, no way would I part with this lovely old lady now. We had been through too much together. We knew each other and responded to each other's every wish. By now it was close to 2 pm and I wanted to make Crisfield by this evening.

The wind was blowing nicely and in just the right direction. The tide drew the current downstream and all the conditions were right. I took the tiller from Arthur and brought the *Sherry D* alongside the Shettles' dock. They jumped off and we bade farewell. It was a wonderful visit and the Shettles are great people. They made me, a stranger, feel right at home and insisted that I return with my wife and offered us the use of the separate cottage guest house with pool. I

The *Bay Bird* with tow. Note that the *Sherry D* is now on the inside of the dock.

promised that I would accept and surely I knew that this was one promise that I would keep.

I started downstream on the next leg of my journey, passing the farm area of the plantation on my way. I noticed off to my port side the large cypress that Arthur had told me to look for on my way out the river. On the wall in the Gun Room was a certificate framed and given to the Shettles by the State of Maryland. The certificate read:

> Bald Cypress (Taxoderem Distichum) determined to have been grown at the time of the American Revolution and declared a Maryland Bicentennial Tree. Est. Age 303 years.

It was a beautiful old tree. I had noticed it on my way up two days before, but I had not realized its age. I knew that I was still in fresh water, as cypress trees do not grow in salt. I had about another three miles to go before I reached the Sound. When I arrived at the mouth of the Pocomoke, just where it makes its final bend into Pocomoke Sound, I found the *Bay Bird* with her long 438-foot tow, blocking the entrance. The tide was not high enough for the *Bay Bird* to get through so they were waiting for the incoming tide. She needed 11 feet, and I wondered what the trick was to get these barges with tows around those narrow bends and especially through the Sound where I, with my 2'4" draft, had touched several times coming in. I dropped my sails and went over to the barge and tied up with the mate's permission. He told me of their predicament and suggested I come aboard and talk to the Captain about the rest of the channel. I walked the length of the barge and boarded the *Bay Bird*.

Capt. Temple Brown, a jolly, young, toothless, one-eyed captain, was a real joy to meet. He claimed I could make it around even though there was only about 10 feet between the barge and a sand spit at Williams Point and, if I got stuck, he would turn the *Bay Bird*, leaving the barge sit where she was, and clear a channel out for me. He then told me the trick of getting through the Sound. What I thought were fishing stakes as I came in were, in actuality, poles installed by the towing company to mark the channel. The captain said that instead of dodging them I should go between them. Capt. Brown was very interested in my trip and said his life's dream was to get a small powerboat and travel, for pleasure, from Long Island to Florida via the Inland Waterway and be able to stop whenever and wherever he wanted. He offered me supplies but I had already stocked up at Cedar Hall. I bade farewell and was wished good luck by the entire crew. They said they would look for me on the Bay. Temple asked me to give him a call when I got into Crisfield to let him know I made it. (He certainly ranked high on my list of the "Good Ole Boys.")

Once past the *Bay Bird*, I raised the main and sailed between the stakes. I was only a few feet out of the channel when "wham," I was on the bottom. How embarrassing! I was only about 300 feet from the tug. There was, however, a good westerly blowing so I pulled in the main, got some speed to the kicker and sailed right off, waving that I was okay.

*Tug **Bay Bird** waits for high water at Williams Point.*

*I have just room enough to go around the **Bay Bird** while Captain Brown and crew watch.*

    I had a great sail into Crisfield and cut through the channel at Broad Creek. There I met my first green head flies of the trip. They were even worse than at Wachapreague in season. By 7 pm I was sailing into Somers Cove in Crisfield, my anchorage for the night, and, to my relief, I found no flies there. I had the last of my Bloody Marys and filled up with crackers and sardines; I was too tired to cook. I also decided not to go ashore but promised myself to return by car someday to tour Crisfield. I called the *Bay Bird* on my VHF Radio and told them I arrived okay. I received a "Roger" followed by a "We'll look for you on the Bay." I then called home on my radio and got a good connection via Point Lookout Marine. By 9:30 pm I was in dreamland but was awakened at midnight by high winds that were knocking the *Sherry D* about. I estimated the winds at 30 knots. After dropping an extra anchor, I returned to bed, thinking about the last two days' experiences. I was getting closer to home how, but I still had some interesting places to see. Tomorrow I would be heading out for Smith Island and then on to Wenona.

CHAPTER 18

Day Twenty-two - Crisfield to Wenona

Monday - June 8th, 1987

I was up at 6:30 am, wanting to get an early start. Planned to sail to Smith Island and then to Wenona today. After hearing the weather forecast, which called for small craft warnings on the Bay, winds gusting from 15 to 25 knots from the north, possible thunderstorms with hail, etc. etc. etc., I went back to my bunk with disgust. (I had had enough of this "bare knuckle" sailing — to use an old salt's expression.) I knew I would never make it up the Bay in that weather.

At 9:30 am, the wind calmed down and I watched the flag at the Coast Guard station drop from horizontal to 45 degrees. I decided to put the main up by itself and took off. I had anchor lines all over the foredeck (which was another good reason to forego using the jib). It turned out to be a beautiful day and, having left Crisfield at 10 am, I was tying up at Smith Island at 1:30 pm after an easy sail. A couple with a little girl and a dog, docked next to me, had sailed over that morning in a 30-foot Cape Dory from Dividing Creek on the western shore. They said there was a real chop and were worried the entire way. Christy, their daughter, got sick, and they really didn't look too happy about being on Smith Island.

I wasn't planning to stay long and went over to Ruke's Restaurant and General Store for a soft crab sandwich and a tall ice tea, the main reason a sailor visits Smith Island. My purchases cost $7.50 and I chalked that up as the price you pay for carrying a camera. Smith Island is a quaint little place with nice people. Similar to Tangier Island where I had been several times before. I met a gentleman also having a soft crab sandwich at Ruke's. He said he was visiting and that he lived in Ocean View, Delaware. I related my experiences going through the Indian River Inlet and he seemed very interested in my trip. He knew the Magnolia Restaurant well and also was a friend of Mrs. Grace Quillen, the retired postmistress of Ocean View and the owner of the B&B where my wife and I had stayed. He was on Smith Island because he owned some property there. It was a business trip.

After my lunch and a quick walk around town, I boarded the *Sherry D* and prepared to depart for Wenona. But, before I left Smith Island, I decided to motor about and take a few pictures from the water. As I passed the old gas dock next to the Pitchcroft Restaurant, there sat my gentleman friend waving as I went by. From previous accounts I had read in the newspapers, I learned that the people who lived here, and had been watermen for generations, were now ready to give in to the developers and agreed to allow luxury condominiums to be built on Smith Island. The Pitchcroft area seemed to stand out in my mind. Was this the property that my friend from Delaware owned?

I have had a concern about the large number of crab pots from the seaside marshes behind the barrier islands all the way up and through this area. There were hundreds and thousands everywhere I sailed. I had read that the female blue crab, toward the end of its second year of life and having mated all over the Bay, migrates in the fall to the high saline waters near the Bay's mouth, while the males winter in the mud of the deep channels. Each female releases millions of eggs, but in this most vulnerable stage, the month or two of larval development after hatching, only a few survive, just enough to maintain a stable population. While this is happening, the male crab hibernates in the deepest mud bottoms of the upper reaches of the Bay and waits for the females to return. The process then continues and, with such obvious fecundity, even with an extremely

The famous Ruke's Restaurant.

The proposed site of new condos on Smith Island.

Crab houses and crab pots on Smith Island.

high mortality among the young, the Bay's crab population continues to grow.

The frightening thing to me was to consider all factors. The over-crabbing as I had seen in my travels; the possibility of a catastrophe that may increase the mortality rate of the larvae causing a decreasing population; and now with the oyster population dwindling due to MSX and dermo, which killed more than 90 percent of the Bay's oysters this past year, I am told that the commercial fishermen are now using their dredges to dig up the male crabs from the deep bottom holes during the winter months.

A waterman's life is difficult enough. But up to this point he stuck it out. It appears that these Islanders, at this time, are fighting a losing battle. With a polluted Bay and its tributaries, fish kills, a diseased oyster crop, a need to over-crab for a growing population and to meet expenses, it is difficult. Still we find this hard-working waterman holding his head high, as if it is all for the love of it. Are we nearing the time when we may see the last oyster, the last crab, and the last waterman? I hope not. Will we soon see condominiums where crab pots once stood? Maybe my old friend from Ocean View hopes so.

*The **Caleb W. Jones** lies to starboard.*

I left Smith Island with the hope that this serene place will remain as nice as it has for the past two hundred years.

At 2 pm I was leaving Smith Island via the western side. I had come in from Crisfield on the eastern side. It was an easy sail from there to Wenona. It was a beautiful day, quite the opposite of what NOAA weather had projected earlier. I arrived at Wenona at 5 pm, just in time to walk around and see some of those famous skipjacks. There sat one in which I was interested, the *Caleb W. Jones*, the first skipjack that Robert de Gast had sailed on.

The evening glow was worth the whole trip.

*The **Sherry D** lies at the end of the old dock.*

Arby Holland.

Dewey Webster had hand carved the tailboard for Robert. That same tailboard is now proudly hanging in Robert's new home. I learned that Dewey had passed away a few years ago. I would not have the chance to meet this fine old gentleman, the last of the tailboard carvers on the Shore. I would have to remember him only as Robert had described in his book, *The Oystermen of the Chesapeake*.

Wenona is a small town with a somewhat rundown harbor, but the people who live there are very friendly and make their living from the Bay. Arby Holland was especially helpful. He owned the local store which sold everything from gasoline to groceries, snacks and hot coffee. Arby puts in a long day at his store, from 5:30 am to 9 pm. A sign on the front of his store says: "Arby's General Store, It ain't the end of the world . . . but you can sure see it from here!" Arby also ran the gas pumps where I docked and said I could lie there, then added "you ain't moving in are ye?" His little son, Joey, rode his bike over and I gave him a tour of the *Sherry D*, which he thought was a pretty little boat (I'm sure I could hire him on in a minute if I were looking for a crew). While looking at the other skipjacks in the harbor, I met another man who suggested I move the *Sherry D* from where she was docked because the chartered fishing boats picked up their passengers there at 5 am. I decided to leave her there as I wanted to get an early start in the morning myself.

Sure enough, before sun up, the fishing and crabbing boats started their engines full throttle. I got up, dressed, had breakfast and said farewell to Arby. He told me he hoped I would come back again soon. He was building a new addition onto his house just behind the store, maybe then it would be finished and I could have dinner with him and his family. I then returned to the *Sherry D* to start another day's adventure.

Good people.

Chapter 19

Day Twenty-three - Wenona to Bloodsworth Island

Tuesday - June 9th, 1987

At 8:30 am I was sailing out of Wenona with the wind blowing a gale right on my nose. I had a reef in the main and had the little working jib up. It took the motor at full throttle to help me buck the waves. Finally, I was out where I could manage a close reach right up to Sharkfin Shoal, stick my arm out, make a left turn into Hooper Strait and then a right into the Honga River. It was an easy course. The wind was blowing hard, there was a heavy chop and I was moving fast. The *Sherry D* held her course well and we sailed with a slight heel to starboard. Once in a while a larger wave would hit the bow and throw us off to leeward, but then my little boat would dig in and come right back on course. She was sailing herself. It was cold and I had on my foul weather gear, zipped up tight, and a life jacket. I was confident and saw no problems.

Wenona was another nice experience, I liked the people there and was glad that I had stopped. As I passed some of the fishing and crabbing boats that were bouncing around as much as I, the people would wave and call to me to have a good trip. These were some of the same people I had met the night before. A few called out for me to be careful as there was a threat of bad storms for tonight. Some of them would wave and then with fist closed and thumb pointing in the air give me a smile and a nod to signify that they approved of my little boat and how nicely she was handling.

I was really proud of myself, and I'm sure that the *Sherry D* was a real beauty as she leaped over the oncoming waves. I also was pleased that these old salts would nod and show their approval. After all, this was the skipjack center of the world. Holland Strait was where these old boys learned to sail, and, if you could sail in these waters and in this kind of weather, you had to be respected. I felt as if I had joined their club and I sailed off leaving them out of sight, with a feeling of jubilation and with the thought that I would be sailing across the Choptank River by tomorrow. Then it happened — I had rounded Sharkfin Shoal Light which by now was way off in the distance. I couldn't find my next marker. I figured that I was about three miles from the Hooper Strait Light, but I couldn't see in the distance. The *Sherry D* was bucking around as if she also knew that something was wrong. There was a wind shift and I had to change off on another tack. I was also in one of those places where I had to go from one chart to another. Trying to find my position on a new chart in a bucking sea, with the spray blowing over the deck, was a real chore. Just keeping my eyeglasses clean was a major problem. It was easy to become disoriented and I was. I did one of the worst things a navigator could do. I trusted my own sense of direction rather than relying on my compass. Way off in the distance, I saw a marker. It was just a pole with a square plaque affixed. I judged it to be about a mile away but couldn't find it on my chart. I sailed for it anyhow hoping that it would give some clue as to where I was. As it turned out, it was another one of those boundary markers. This time it separated Somerset County from Dorchester County. It is not unusual to find these markers in the southern Maryland-northern Virginia waters as trading rights, ownership, and water boundaries have been disputed in this area from about 1634 to the present day. Robert de Gast gives an interesting account of this in his book, *Western Wind Eastern Shore*.

I must have sailed in circles for a long time, tacking first in one direction and then another. Then a larger sailboat, off in the distance, was coming in from what I thought was the Bay, and it appeared that she was heading for the area of Chance on Deale Island which I had passed earlier. (Later, I found that she was actually heading up the Nanticoke River.) I thought it would be a good idea to follow the route that she had come from. That didn't work either, as it required still another tack; and then I even lost sight of that boat. The wind was picking up stronger now and the sky became overcast. I knew that I had to do something in a hurry or I would be in real trouble. Had I been in control of myself, this would have been the time to settle down, collect my wits and regain confidence in my compass. Instead, I fought to just keep sailing my little boat.

Finally, I saw a lone fisherman in a small open boat at anchor and I sailed over toward him. As I got closer, I could see that he looked like one of the old timers in the area; but he was also having problems of his own. He couldn't get his engine started, and he seemed even more excited than I. He looked up and saw me, and cried out, "HELP!" I tried to sail to him, but he was in shallow water. Fortunately, the skies began to clear and the wind slackened some, but the old fisherman was still excited and called to me to ask if I could see "Them thar fishing boats way off in the distance?" Yes, I could see them. There were about three or four of them. He said for me to sail quickly over there and tell them to come get him. They were his friends. Well, I thought I might just as well. I couldn't be any worse off, and this fellow didn't appear to be of any help. I was about 50 yards from him, coming about to head for the fishing fleet, when I ran aground. The tide was going out at this time, and it was Oyster all over again. I guess the old fisherman didn't know about sailboats, because he was having a fit. He couldn't understand why I wasn't moving, and I had the impression that he thought I could just get up and go. He called to me to ask if I had any flares, and I called back that I had three. He shouted, "Well fire the damn things!" I fired two and blew my fog horn five blasts to give the danger signal. Nothing happened, and by then the fishing fleet had disappeared. They were gone.

Well, there we were, what a pair! — he with engine trouble and me hard aground. The tide was running out strong and the sky would haze over, then clear, and then haze over again. The wind blew hard again, and the sky was very black to the east. I was listing hard now to port, as the water shallowed under my hull. I had less than a foot of water, and the keel was down in the soft ooze. The fisherman worked frantically on his motor, and I could hear him swearing and cursing. Every once in a while he would give it a good kick, and then shout from the pain in his foot. All of a sudden the engine started, and the old guy pulled up his anchor in a hurry and headed my way with an offer to pull me off. Then he hit bottom but could back off. He was too far away to throw me a line, however. I shouted back to him that it was of no use. I was too hard aground now, and he couldn't pull me off even if he could get to me. He was still very excited and said he had to go, but I could see that he was very concerned about leaving me there and he offered to send help — he knew my position. I declined the offer and said I would just wait for the tide to come in and then float off. I did, however, think to ask him directions to the Honga River. He shouted, as he was backing off, that I would have to "go all the way around that thar island with the tower on it and past Sharkfin Shoal Light, about seven miles." At this point, I was more confused than ever, and the fisherman left in a hurry. I knew that I would be here for a while and settled back to wait for the tide to come back in.

All of a sudden it turned very black, the wind blew harder and it became very cold, with thunder and lightning off in the distance. Thank God I was aground. My sails were down and furled, and I had things pretty much organized and ready for bad weather. Had I still been sailing, this wind would have ripped the sails right off the *Sherry D* and probably would have taken my rigging also. I turned on the radio, a little nervous about attracting lightning with the antenna, and heard that there was a tornado alert. It had already set down in Franklin City, Virginia. (This was the Franklin City near Wallops Island.) I knew that wasn't far from me and I realized that the black sky that I had

I fired two.

All of a sudden it turned black.

seen earlier could have been the funnel. The old fisherman must have seen it also, which may explain why he was so excited and wanted to get out of there, and is probably why the fishing fleet disappeared rather than coming to our assistance.

Some months later after I returned home, I learned from my friend Jim Dykes (the dairy farmer that I met on Assawoman Island and also on the Pocomoke) that he had returned to our spot on Assawoman Island with some friends and his wife to vacation a little and had set up a camp site. Jim told me that he had never been so frightened in all his life since his tour in Vietnam where he had been caught in a mortar attack. This storm had reminded him of the same experience. There was no place to go; the wind had lifted their tent right off them and had blown it away. There was nothing they could do but to lie there, grip their hands into the dunes, and hang onto each other waiting for it to blow over. They had seen the funnel and watched three rockets from the site on Wallops Island being accidentally launched by lightning. (They had to be destroyed in mid-air.)

I read an account of this in the June 13, 1987, *Eastern Shore News*, titled "Lightning accidentally launches NASA rockets." Part of the account read, "At 7:05 pm, lightning struck the launch area and the three rockets launched themselves. Witnesses saw only a flash. All three rockets dropped into the water — the 16-foot-long Orion about 300 to 500 feet offshore and the two four-foot testing rockets about 2.5 miles out." This must have been what my friend and his companions had seen.

There was really not much I could do either. I was hard aground, laid over on my side. The sky was black and the wind whistled in the rigging. The lightning cracked and the thunder rumbled. Prior to my departure, I had made a chain with a snap hook to attach to the back stay and throw overboard for a ground in case of electrical storms. I remembered its being in the lazarette. I didn't know how much good it would do, but now was a good time to try it out. No sooner had I thrown the chain overboard and watched it sink in less than a foot of water, than a wall of rain came across the sound. Just in time, I was able to slide into the cabin and close the hatch. The next thing to do was to disconnect the radio antenna, then wait and wonder if the lightning, which was striking all around, would follow down the loose wire dangling there in the cabin. If it did, then maybe my radio, at least, would survive.

The rain beat on the hull and the cabin top, and though my *Sherry D* lay in only one foot of water, the waves beat upon the hull with such force it appeared that the boat would lift right off the bottom and then

*The **Sherry D** laid over on her port side. Thank God I was aground.*

bang down again a few feet farther to lee. There was nothing that I could do but ride it out and take whatever came. I lay there in the lower port side bunk that formed a V with that side of the hull. It was difficult to get out of the bunk. Each time I tried, a wave would hit and I would fall right back down into the V.

There was plenty of time to think, and I wondered again where I was and how I got there. This was surely Bloodsworth Island and I had read the chapter in John Barth's *The Sot-Weed Factor* not long ago, about Ebenezer Cooke, when he was caught in a vicious storm much like this one. Of course, Barth's tale took place in the 1600s, and Ebenezer had sailed across the Bay from St. Mary's City with Captain Cairn in his gaff-rigged sloop not forty feet long with a 3½-foot draft. The storm had washed them ashore on Bloodsworth Island, and Ebenezer Cooke had stated in the book that, "he attributes only to the violence of the storm, and more especially to the purgative ordeal of the three hours dancing on the doormat of extinction, could he offer any affection for those who betrayed him." Though I knew of no one who betrayed me, I felt much the same. If there had been such a person, then this would be the time that I would be willing to forgive and forget.

It was my guess that I was somewhere just south of Hooper's Island in the area that John Barth's Captain Cairn had called "Limbo Straits." I had the good fortune to have sailed into the cove at the north end of Bloodsworth Island that the good captain had called Okahanikan, where they ran for shelter rather than take their chances with the surf on the Dorset mainland.

As a matter of interest, and as I rewrite this account, I recall another incident that occurred in the spring of 1988, when the skipjack *Clarence Crockett* hit one of the county markers separating Somerset County and Dorchester County. Oddly enough, Captain Paul Holland, skipper of the *Clarence Crockett*, was the brother of my storekeeper friend Arby, in Wenona, and was returning from oystering up on the Magothy River, my home waters, when she hit the boundary marker that I think had caused me to become disoriented just one year and a month before. The 80-year-old ship was one of those that I had seen in Wenona and was chosen as a symbol of Maryland on a U.S. commemorative postage stamp. She sank in about 10 feet of water on March 17th, 1988. Captain Holland and his two crewmen spent 14 hours in freezing weather clinging to the marker the skipjack hit before they were spotted and rescued by the Department of Natural Resources Police.

This Bloodsworth Island was rightly named, maybe by Captain John Smith, as I understand that he also ran into a few incidents here. It was no cup of tea to sail. I thought again about John Barth's Captain Cairn and his gaff-rigged sloop as her keel had brushed the bottom. The captain dropped his anchor and came up into the wind. It was then that Ebenezer cried, "can it be we're safe?" With this, Captain Cairn repeated an old proverb, "and only a dead man is safe from death." This came to mind as I lay there taking the pounding on the shallow oyster-bed bottom. Was this a dream in which I would drown before I awoke? I was sure it was not a dream as it was too real, but I took comfort in the thought that the storm would soon be over. Fortunately, the severity of these storms rarely last more than

*Perhaps the last photos taken of the **Clarence Crockett** before she sank in March, 1988.*

*Commemorative stamp featuring the **Clarence Crockett**.*

an hour. I was glad that I was on the bottom and close to shore, where I could be found, rather than in the open Bay.

It was close to 7:30 pm, when the rain, the lightning and the thunder ceased. The wind was still blowing hard, but I was at least able to come out of my sheltered cabin. The wind and the waves churned the water white, and the *Sherry D* was still on her side. I held my portable wind meter up and clocked 40-45 knots. Then I retrieved my camera from the cabin where I had it tied and hanging from one of the hand-hold rails. I couldn't pass up a shot of the sky and the mast showing the angle of heel. The angle of heel was due to the *Sherry D* lying on the bottom, but I was convinced that, had I been in open deep water, the angle of heel with only a bare pole would have been even more severe.

There was not much daylight left, and I knew that I would be here for the night. I had to know where I was, and the old fisherman's directions confused me more than I had been previously. To follow his route would take me right back from where I had come. It just didn't make sense, and I was still unable to find myself on the charts. My compass didn't help, as I had no reference points but a tower and a house that I couldn't even find on the charts. It was time to get the radio working and I re-connected the antenna. I called and called the Honga River Marine Police thinking that they would be the closest station. If I was in Okahanikan Cove, which was my best guess, then the Honga River should be only about three to four miles north and across Hooper Strait. Robert de Gast had talked about a nice experience that he had with the Marine Police up in the Wicomico, and my charts showed a Maryland Natural Resources Police Patrol (MNRP) at the swing bridge that I would be heading for off the Honga. I received no answer, so

I called the Coast Guard on channel 16. Again, I received no reply. Then I tried, "any station, any station, this is *Sherry D*, this is *Sherry D*, WTQ 2714, over." All of a sudden to my surprise I received a reply. "*Sherry D* this is the fishing boat *Mary Kate*, over." The captain turned out to be a fisherman who had been listening to my transmissions and asked if he could help. We switched to channel 68 and I explained my situation, telling him that I was okay but still aground which was a good thing because of the storm. This fellow spoke as if he knew what he was doing and appeared very calm in his questioning. He asked what were the last markers I had seen before running aground, and I told him about the boundary marker and about the tower and the lone house on the opposite shore. He finally came back and said that he knew these waters very well and didn't think that I was where I thought I was. He recommended that we contact the Coast Guard. He was in range and would relay for me. I was to stand by on channel 16. It quickly became clear to me that this unknown fisherman did know what he was doing. He gave me the impression, by his voice and his reactions to my situation, that he was one who knew the responsibility of the bridge of the ship in a storm. For this, I was appreciative.

    I could hear him call Coast Guard Station Crisfield, and then I heard, on my radio, their conversation. The fisherman explained that he was in contact with a lone sailor in a small sailboat that had just weathered the passing storm. He further explained that I was aground and could not determine my position; that I was not able to raise the Marine Police or the Coast Guard on channel 16, and that he would relay for us. I sat there monitoring their conversation with great satisfaction and then I heard the fisherman say, "I have been working these waters for many years and think that I know his approximate location. If he is where I think he is (in Holland Strait), I wouldn't want to be there on a night like this. I strongly recommend you make contact."

    The Coast Guard Station acknowledged and asked the fisherman to tell me to switch to channel 22 and try to call them. He contacted me again to relay those instructions, and I informed him that I was able to monitor his conversation and that I was switching to channel 22. I thanked him for his help and his concern. He replied, "I'm switching to channel 22 also and will monitor your calls till I know that you have good contact." This we did and I called the Coast Guard Station Crisfield. They came back loud and clear. I guess that I was a little excited and tried immediately to tell them my predicament. At this time the Coast Guard operator did not seem concerned but went on in a very cool voice asking me a series of questions. My name, the boat's name, registration number, sail number, type of boat, my phone number, date of birth, etc., etc. When he asked the name, address and phone number of my next of kin, I began to worry. In actuality, I realized that these questions were necessary and the operator was filling out a form. As we talked, the station must have been honing in on my position, perhaps by triangulation, because my questioner came back with,

    "We have you located, do you want us to send a patrol craft to pick you up? We could be there within a half hour."

My reply was, "Thanks very much, but I don't think you could reach me. It is too shallow, over."

Coast Guard replied, "I guess you're right, over."

I went on to explain that I was fine and would have to wait for the tide to lift me off the bottom. What I really needed at this time was to know where to move for deeper water when the tide did come in. The Coast Guard operator said "wait one" and then came back with,

"The tide will be max high at 11:35 pm and I should move about 500 yards southeast. I would anchor there, in about six feet of water, for the night, and then leave by daylight the next morning."

They had fixed my position just north of Spring Island in the Holland Straits. The tower I saw was on Northeast Island and the house on Adams Island. How I got there I will never know. I was not at the north end of Bloodsworth Island but was at the south end. I checked my charts and sure enough, there I lay in two feet of water. My old fishing, engine-kicking friend was right. In order to get to the Honga River I had to sail all the way around that "thar" island about seven miles. The only thing I could think of was, when I had rounded Sharkfin Shoal Light, that wind shift sent me flying south, backtracking my previous course, and I came around the lower island through the Gunbarrel; and that's when I saw my old fishing friend.

I made up my mind that I would pass up the Honga River this trip. I was not about to try that again. The Coast Guard plotted a course for me to follow in the morning. They recommended that I sail south about four miles giving Holland Island a good berth. There was a long sandbar to the south but if I was careful, I could cut across. It would be low tide at that time again, but at least it would be coming in. I should pick up Holland Island Bar Light, round it, and then head north up the Bay side of Bloodsworth Island. They further went on to tell me that I could expect a rough night. It would be clear skies with a bright moon, but very high winds. They recommended we maintain a radio check every hour on the hour throughout the night. It was about 9:30 pm, and I would check in with my first call at 10 pm. This station would be going off duty after 10 pm, and, after that, I would call Coast Guard Group Eastern Shore. Sure enough, this worked out fine and at 11 pm the Group Eastern Shore knew all about me. They were glad that I was okay, as they had another sailboat up on the Nanticoke River that was also aground. If they hadn't heard, they would have sent a helicopter out to look for me. I take it that the other sailboat was the one that I had seen earlier in the day.

As the Coast Guard had said, the tide would be high at 11:30 pm. It was just about that time when I could feel the keel bump on the bottom with each wave. Of course the *Sherry D* had been righting herself for some time. Right about 11:30 pm I went up on deck and found the moon big and bright. Big white clouds rolled across the sky and hazed over the brightness for a while, it was a pretty sight. The wind had slackened some but was enough to pitch a few white caps upon the sea. I put the motor in the motor well and pulled the cord. She started right off and I swung the bow around to 135 degrees on the compass. I had a lead line and I put a knot in it at six feet. Then I moved slowly, dropping the lead line as I went. It was hard to determine 500 yards and I knew that, when I was in six feet of water, it was time to drop the anchor. This I did and let out all of the anchor line I had, about 150 feet. All was fine and it was now midnight, time for my check-in. I told the Eastern Shore Group what I had done and that I was pretty tired and was going to get some sleep. I would set my alarm; but, if I slept through it, not to worry as I was in good shape now. I also needed to turn my radio off, as I had no way to charge my battery and I thought it was getting low. I received an "affirmative, and out." The boat bounced around a little, but in no time I was asleep.

It seemed as if I had just dozed off when I awoke with a start. Actually, it was just after 3 am. I had missed my last three radio checks. The little boat was bouncing around like mad and the wind-driven water was crashing against the sides and cabin top, beating at my door. There was a very unusual sound like the flapping of the rotary blades of a helicopter. My first reaction was that the Coast Guard had sent a 'copter to look for me, due to the absence of my radio checks. I grabbed a flashlight and slid back the cabin hatch. Just about that time a large wave came crashing over the deck and right down the hatch. I tried to slam the hatch cover shut, but it was too late, I was soaked. I stuck my head out of the hatch to see what was going on and took another splash right in the face. Forward, I could see that both of my jibs were running right up the forestay. They were flapping and beating themselves together and sounded worse than any helicopter blades I had ever heard. I had to do something or I would lose my two important sails.

Why I did this I do not know, since I was already soaked, but I threw on my foul weather gear and a life jacket, connected the life line and proceeded to crawl up and over the cabin top. At one point, a wave hit the boat broadside, rolled her over and threw me to the deck. I lay there on the deck and then, on my belly, I pulled myself forward, hanging on for dear life. When I reached the bow, I was barely able to hang onto the pulpit, as the bow would submerge and a wave would come crashing right over me and the whole boat. I did have the foresight, when I came out of the hatchway, to close it again, otherwise the entire boat would have been flooded. The jibs were quivering, flapping and banging as they had just about reached the top of the mast.

What had happened was that I had the two jibs tied down to the deck with shock cord. The wind and the waves apparently got under the sails and stretched the elastic cords, eventually breaking them under the strain. The working jib was snapped to the forestay; to secure the genoa, I had also shackled its head to the forestay. When the working jib started its path upward, it took the big genoa right along with it. The jib sheets had pulled out of their blocks and whipped back and forth, giving me an unmerciful lashing. I was able to hang onto the pulpit with one hand and with the other I pulled down on the jib. All the while, the bow would rise and fall while a wave would wash over the deck and me.

Once I had the two jibs down, I was able to roll over and lie on them while, with one hand pulling in the jib sheets which were now in the water. With them, I lashed the jibs back down to the deck. There was now no order to anything. Just tie it down, I thought. I grabbed every line I could find and worked my way back over the cabin top, wrapping lines around anything that might move. I even took the mainsail sheet and wrapped it around the boom and the furled sail, down to the hand rails on the cabin top, and then to the mast. The next thing I noticed was that, with each rise of the bow, the boat would back a few more feet. It occurred to me that, if that anchor pulled out of the bottom (or worse, if the anchor rode should break), then my boat and I both would be spending the rest of the night in the comfort of that house in Adams Island. There was another anchor with 12 feet of chain and 150 feet of anchor line in the cabin. I was able to retrieve that and again made my way to the foredeck dragging the anchor out. There was no way I could throw the anchor, so I just lowered it over the opposite side of the bow from the other anchor and coiled the line in ripcord fashion like a parachute riser. Then I tied the end to the mast. If something should happen to the already set anchor, the boat would certainly drift back and the anchor would pull the 150 foot ripcord out. Feeling a little more secure, I made my way back to the cabin, got out of the wet clothes and back into my sleeping bag. I was exhausted.

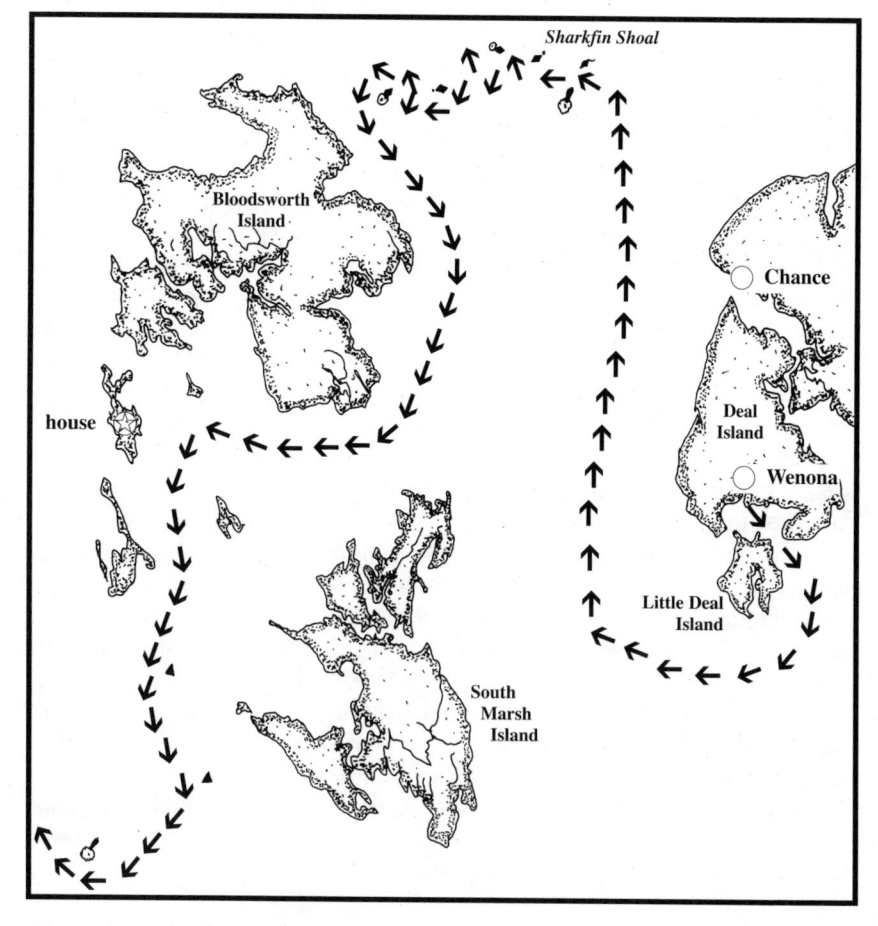

Chapter 20

Day Twenty-four – Bloodsworth Island to Solomons Island

Wednesday - June 10th, 1987

Last night was a rough one, and I was still very tired. It was now 5:30 am and the sun was just peeking through the port lights. Curiosity got the better of me, and I wanted to see how far I moved during the night. I opened the hatch, stood in the companionway and looked out. It was still hazy, and the wind, though slackened a little, was still creating white caps across the water. It was much stronger than I had hoped for. I hadn't moved very much, and there was the house on Adams Island and the tower on the opposite shore just as it was before dark last night. The little boat was a mess. Everything below was wet and thrown around. I climbed up on deck to retrieve my whisker pole that was lying crosswise, but tied, over the foredeck. As I picked it up, I laughed at myself and wondered what any of these old fishermen would think if they came by and saw me here like this. Had the *Sherry D*'s hull been painted white, she would have looked like Moby Dick with all the lines wrapped about her; and with me standing there on the foredeck with the whisker pole in hand like a harpoon. I could easily have been mistaken for Captain Ahab.

It was time for a little breakfast, so I pumped up the air pressure in my one-burner stove, made a large pot of coffee, and prepared bacon, eggs and cereal. How my eggs survived, I will never know. While having this great breakfast, I realized that I really hadn't eaten anything but a peanut butter and jelly sandwich since yesterday morning. This also reminded me that I had best prepare my peanut butter and jelly sandwiches for lunch today. This time I packed four sandwiches, a full thermos of hot coffee, a couple of apples and some moon pies that I had bought at Arby Holland's store in Wenona. It looked as if this would be another one of those long, tedious days. I had previously checked in with the Coast Guard and told them my status. I further stated that, "I would depart soon and take their recommendation to go south through Holland Strait and then out to the Bay to Holland Island Bar Light before turning north."

This would add another 12 miles to my trip and, for the *Sherry D*, about another half day sailing if I had to tack. The way the winds were blowing, this would be the case. The Coast Guard duty officer said that he would appreciate it if I would notify the Baltimore District when I arrived back in the Magothy. They would relay a message to Baltimore that I was on my way north and that they could plot my course. If I needed help again while in their area, I was not to hesitate to call. I thanked him and told him I really appreciated his concern and expertise. I followed this up with a request, that if they again had contact with the captain of the *Mary Kate*, to please extend my thanks to him. We signed off.

There was still a lot to do before I could depart. The wind was blowing about 20 knots, and I reefed the mainsail a third of the sail. Of course, I had to untie all the lines that I had used during the night, and I re-furled the head sails, tying the big genoa down on deck but setting the little working jib, ready to put up when needed. I had two anchors out, each with 150 feet of line. It was a good thing that I had lowered the second anchor to the bottom last night, as that was the one holding. My ripcord effect must have worked, as 150 feet of line had passed through the chock, and the 1/2-inch nylon line was stretched tight where the other rode was slack.

Once the anchor was up, I left the line gathered on the deck; the bow turned to the south, and I hurried back to the cockpit to take over the tiller. The mainsail blew all the way out to port as the north wind pushed us from behind. I was passing the south end of Holland Island in no time and the expanse of water on out to the Bay was so wide that I had a tendency to cut across on a westerly course to the Bay. My charts showed this to be all shallow water and I was not looking forward to any more mishaps. My better judgment told me now to continue south and I did, until I was in Kedges Straits that separates South Marsh Island from Smith Island — the area known as Solomons Lump. I had passed this spot two days earlier when I sailed from Smith Island to Wenona; but now Smith was way off to the southeast, and I made my turn west towards Holland Island Bar Light.

The wind was coming from the north, which meant I had to tack if I was to go north up the Bay. I decided to stay on my westerly course for a while in order to give me a wider berth off Bloodsworth Island. Finally, I came about and took a port tack hoping to sail parallel to the island, but the wind kept pushing me in closer and closer to Bloodsworth. There was another tower on the Island. This one was clearly on the Bayside. My charts showed, just to the north of me, "Prohibited Area" and "Danger Area, Unexploded Ordinance." When I saw a helicopter fly over, land on the island next to the tower and drop a couple of men off, I thought, *"uh oh, I'm in the wrong spot again, soon a few planes would be flying over to bomb me."* Actually, Bloodsworth Island is an uninhabited bombing range, and I thought perhaps these fellows might be the forward observers.

It was time to come about again, and this time I just kept going west across the Bay. It seemed to take forever to cross over to the western shore. I had raised the working jib, and the Bay was getting rough again. I was tired but had to keep going. Soon I saw a lighthouse that I recognized as Point No Point Light. The sun came out strong, but the wind and waves became stronger also. My boat was really bouncing around, and I would find myself dropping off to sleep once in a while. I was sailing, but not making much headway. The winds were blowing a gale again and the waves created a real chop. I was just now starting to cross the main ships' channel. Point No Point Light was still about five miles off and Point Lookout, at the mouth of the Potomac, was about 10 miles to my southwest. I was really tired, and I didn't know if my lack of speed was due to my poor sailing, bucking the currents, or the boat being knocked around by the waves which

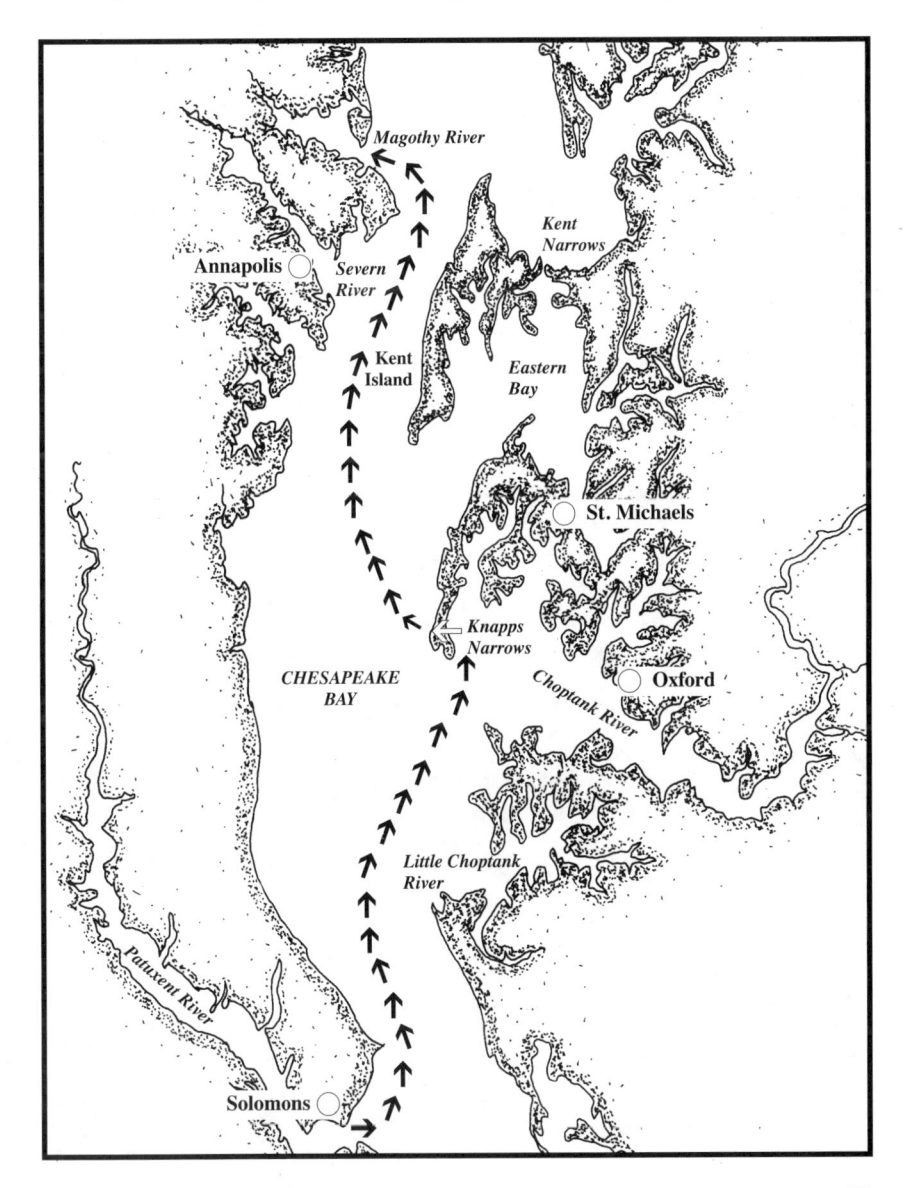

appeared now to be about three to four feet. Possibly, it could be a combination of all. I was in the middle of nowhere and a good day's sail to any quiet harbor. Nothing to do, but just keep going. I tried playing my Palauan tapes, drinking coffee and then, finally, I let the *Sherry D* sail herself again while I went below to check the marine radio and weather. I found the boat did much better by herself than with me hanging on to the tiller.

The weather forecast was much the same, but the forecaster was announcing 10 to 15 knots southeasterly winds with one to two-foot waves at the mouth of the Potomac, no chance of rain and skies were clearing. That was the only thing he had right, as just ten miles north I was experiencing 15 to 20 knot winds from the north and two to four-foot waves. I played with my radio for a while and ran across the marine telephone operator. It was always fun to listen in on someone else's conversations. I know that it is not nice to eavesdrop, but — what the heck, I had nothing else to do. I heard a call from another sailor, to his wife in Washington, DC. Apparently, he was then sailing a forty-foot something or other up the Potomac and had planned to arrive home that evening. He and another fellow had sailed this boat from Bermuda, leaving there about a week prior and had some really rough ocean sailing. They thought they were glad to enter the mouth of the Chesapeake yesterday morning, but went on to fight rough seas all the way up the Bay.

I gather that there were two men on board, as the caller kept referring to "his friend" (I can't remember his name) as taking turns at the wheel and watch. It was when they reached the mouth of the Potomac early this morning that they didn't think they'd make it. They were ready to go back to ocean sailing. They had just passed Smith Point Light in the wee hours of the morning and started

Anchored submarine off the Patuxent firing range.

The old Cedar Point Lighthouse.

Just in time for the Wednesday night races.

their approach up the Potomac when they ran head on to some of the roughest weather either of them had ever experienced. The wind must have been coming right out of the Potomac. This was about the same time that I had experienced my turmoil behind Bloodsworth Island with the winds taking my two headsails up the forestay. I couldn't help but take interest in this conversation, and it reaffirmed my experiences. I was pretty worn out after fighting these storms for about 19 days now and in such a small boat. I was glad to hear that others felt the same.

Sometime later, after I was home, I attended another of my sailing club's meetings and this time the guest speaker was Patricia Kearns, a very knowledgeable and unusual person. Unusual, because, as a woman, she is a marine surveyor, and a very good one. After hearing her speak, I realized that if I ever needed a marine survey again I would call on her. Ms. Kearns subject was "Safety at Sea." Apparently, she does a lot of marine surveying for insurance companies and is very knowledgeable about conditions one should expect to encounter while sailing these beautiful waters. She went on to tell us that "she has sailed, and sailed single-handedly, over 10,000 miles of ocean sailing. Much of this mileage has been in heavy seas, but the most vicious and frightening was right here in our own Chesapeake Bay, right off the mouth of the Potomac River." As she spoke, I recalled the conversation I had heard over my marine radio, and I wish that I had contacted that vessel to find out who they were and more about their experience. I'm sure that they would like to relate their tale to Ms. Kearns.

Well, I kept sailing and, after another peanut butter and jelly sandwich, I came about and was able to head north. The wind had now calmed a little and changed around to the northeast. I was able to pull my sails in tight, and I sailed close hauled right up the western shore, through the Patuxent firing range area, past the anchored submarine and the old deteriorated Cedar Point Lighthouse. It was about 4 pm now and the best and nearest anchorage I knew of was Mill Creek up in the Patuxent and close to Solomons Island. It was not my intention to hit the western shore on this trip as I started out to follow the de Gast route. Well, as it was, I did see about all of the areas that Robert de Gast had photographed and written about, but I didn't see them with the serenity and tranquillity in all cases that Robert had found. My voyage had taken on a different slant and I saw no harm in shooting for the rest stop. It was Mill Creek and I made a hard port turn and headed up the Patuxent River. It was another eight miles, or about two hours for me. I put the little kicker in the motor well and pulled the cord. By wind and fuel, I made good time.

Soon after passing Drum Point, I saw a fleet of sailboats all jockeying for racing position, and I heard the five-minute starting gun. If I hurried, I would be in a good position for the start of the Solomons Island Wednesday night races. Instead of entering, I sailed right on through. However, I did stay out of their way, having done enough racing in my day to know that I must give right of way to the racing pennant. I did get a few dirty looks from a couple of these well-tuned, spit and polished hulls, as their masters looked down on this beat-up old lady with a haggard sailor at her tiller. Little did they know what we had accomplished in these past few days.

Finally, I rounded the point and followed the water going up into St. Thomas Creek, and then off to the right into Mill Creek where I had anchored so many times before in my Sabre that I had sailed back and forth from the Magothy to the Rappahannock. It was a beautiful little cove, and now it was waiting for me. It was a "slick ca'm." It was time to drop anchor, and I did. I dropped the sails and took only a wrap around them to hold the main off the cabin top. The working jib just lay on the deck. I put the little engine in reverse to take a bite into the bottom with the anchor and then shut it off, leaving it hanging in the motor well. I then picked up the radio microphone, switched to channel 26 and called the marine telephone operator. I gave her my home telephone number. It was a quick call to say that I was OK and where I was. I signed off, dropped on my bunk and did not awaken till the next morning.

It was a "slick ca'm" at my little cove in Mill Creek.

CHAPTER 21

Day Twenty-five - Mill Creek to Knapps Narrows

Thursday - June 11th, 1987

It is 8:30 am and I overslept. My alarm was set for 7 am, but apparently I slept through its low buzz. It is a beautiful morning, weather report says light SSW winds and only 40 percent chance of thunderstorms this afternoon. I feel that home is just around the corner, and although this has been one exciting and adventurous trip, I'm looking forward to home. I think these last few days have gotten to me, and I look forward to the remaining beautiful part of the Chesapeake. I want to work my way back to the Eastern Shore, across the Choptank and up through Knapps Narrows. Even though I feel close, I still have about 75 miles to go. That's a lot to squeeze into a little boat that only averages four and a half knots. However, my experience indicated that when winds are favorable I can get six to six and a half knots. Now that's moving for any sailboat!

I looked around, and realized how much I had to do before starting. Things were in a mess and, in fact, there was much more to do than just the regular tidying up.

I went to the foredeck to take the kerosene anchor light down and decided it was time to give that poor little working jib a rest. She had done a good job. I switched to the large genoa and raised it to check for any tears, etc. I'm sure that even though she only lay on the foredeck for most of the past week, she didn't get much sleep either. Most of the time she was splashed and drenched with salt water, wind blown around the tied down extra gas tanks, and dragged in the sea while lashed to the forward pulpit. All was fine, and she would be perfect for today. I did, however, leave the working jib in her place on the foredeck, ready to go up if need be. I did not want to be careless this close to home.

Now some breakfast. Cold cereal, a hard boiled egg and coffee. Maybe I can leave by 10 am.

While changing head sails, I saw a Sabre 28, *Irish Mist*, heading out. She must have been anchored up the creek. Probably heading for Oxford and the Sabre

World Cup Regatta. That's where I would have been heading had it not been for some of the delays on this trip. I waved, and received a wave in return, but I'm sure the skipper of the *Irish Mist* did not recognize me.

While drying things out at Mill Creek, some ducks knocked on my door. I can never turn down a hungry mouth and broke out some of the last of my bread.

At 11 am I was just getting ready to pull up anchor from this lovely cove. I planned to stop at a marina that I could see from there to get some ice and fresh water, which I needed badly.

The Solomons Marina was very handy and I bought some ice. An elderly, heavy-set man was cleaning up the dock and helped me with my lines. He had a cap on that said, "I'm Grumpy." He pressed a buzzer and helped me with a hose to put water in my tank. Soon a nice-looking, high school-age girl came out and sold me some ice. The bill was $1.75 and I handed her a $2.00 bill and said to keep the change. She said, "Oh no, sir, that wouldn't be right," and walked all the way to the end of the dock to get my 25¢ change. When she left, I kidded with Grumpy that I offered the girl a tip because I had been out to sea too long and she was pretty; he was just a grumpy old man. I handed him my quarter change and another 50¢ to boot. He would not take it, and said he "didn't do nothin' to earn it." He laughed and said "I jus' like people who come in. It's my pleasure to help out." I told him he wasn't a grumpy old man and that I was just kidding. He was "All Smiles." I think he liked that name.

I left the marina at noon and soon had my sails up. It was a beautiful day, a nice eight-knot southeasterly wind and I was out past the Calvert Cliffs in no time. A beautiful broad reach — the type of sailing that my wife Sherry likes and, I must admit, that I also like. I took off my long trousers and put my shorts on, removed my shirt and doused myself with suntan lotion. This was the best sail that I had since the run from Cape Charles to Nassawadox Creek, and that was on the 4th of June. Today is the 11th. I calculated that three-fourths of my time out had been really rough sailing and, if I had it to do over, I would choose this same boat. If there was anything wrong in her sailing ability it must have been my fault and not the *Sherry D*'s. She's a real beauty and, if it is at all possible, a real friend. We kind of look out for each other, and I try my best to keep her in good repair.

I calculated that I would sail 32 miles to Knapps Narrows and it would be another 17 miles to Tilghman Point where I planned to anchor. My ETA at Knapps Narrows was 8 pm. Maybe I would stay there.

I passed the deep-water port for the super-tankers, B&G Power Plant, Calvert Cliffs and took a reading of 30 degrees right to the Knapps Narrows and the north side of the Choptank. It was a straight shot and I wing-and-winged it three-fourths of the way. A nice sail, but I had to really watch the tiller as with a following sea the boat wanders.

The Eastern Shore looked so close; why did it take so long to get across in that blow yesterday? There were more sails out here than crab boats on the eastern side. Some going north, some going south. I noticed a lot of Sabres, a one-design class — I myself own a Sabre 34. I tried to get them on the radio, as I was sure

Sunset at Knapps Narrows.

Bascule bridge at Knapps Narrows, Tilghman Island.

that they were heading for Oxford and the Sabre World Cup Regatta. Finally in the Choptank I made contact with the *Isolandic*, a Sabre 34 just like my *Brigadoon*. The crew on her was from Pennsylvania and were sailing her for the owner who would meet them in Oxford for the regatta. They had been to Block Island last year and talked about what a great time they had. I told them a little about my trip and to tell Roger Hewson, the President of Sabre Yachts, and a great guy, that I would surely have had the *Brigadoon* there if I had not been delayed. I wished him another good and successful regatta. The crew member said he copied everything and would get the message through.

I had a beautiful breeze and beat my ETA by over 2 hours (of course when I calculated my ETA, I estimated 4 knots, and actually I was averaging 5 knots). I went straight through the bascule bridge with no trouble. The bridge tender was really on the ball and I think he even judged the current for me. I had come about just before entering the Narrows and dropped my sails. I motored through and it worked well. Just on the other side of the bridge, I saw the Bay Hundred Restaurant with a dock and gas pumps. I thought about those good Tilghman Island crab cakes that I had heard so much about, and decided right then and there — "dinner out tonight." This should be my last night out, and I deserved it.

Jamie Monahan and his wife, a nice young couple who owned the restaurant, said it was still a long way to Tilghman Point and I could stay there at the gas dock tonight. No charge. The crab cakes were good and it was a really nice restaurant, I could eat dinner there also. I did and it was a treat. I had a chance to talk to the Monahans and promised I would return in the fall for oysters.

Tomorrow I should be going under the Bay Bridge and, if all goes well, into the Magothy late in the afternoon. The weather is calling for showers and thunderstorms. We'll see what tomorrow brings. I've decided not to go into Eastern Bay and Kent Narrows. I remembered that tomorrow is Friday and the bridge opens only on special hours because of traffic. I didn't want to take the chance of getting stuck.

Chapter 22

Day Twenty-six - Knapps Narrows to Magothy River

Friday - June 12th, 1987

Last night was not bad. I stayed tied to the gas dock at the Bay Hundred Restaurant. The bridge kept opening all night. This must be the busiest bridge tender on the Eastern seaboard, and he is really on his toes. Opens right on time. He must get a lot of practice.

I was hoping for another good night's sleep but awoke with all kinds of bites. I had failed to put screens in because there was a nice breeze and I wasn't bothered when I went to bed. Uh Oh! The no-see'ums had arrived. I doused myself with "Skin So Soft," and after awhile, that seemed to do the trick. I hoped none of those old fishermen would come to check me out. They would really wonder who this is, smelling so sweet.

I turned the radio on this morning and got Dick Ireland and FM 102 WLIF. I knew I was close to home. The first report was of an accident at Jumpers Hole Road and Route 2. Now I knew I was back home and again close to the real world. After departing Knapps Narrows, I changed to the small jib and full main. Winds reported out of southwest, 12 to 15 knots. Should be another nice reach. I would be going up behind Poplar Island to Bloody Point Light.

Bloody Point Light.

The weather radio was right again. The winds were beautiful southwest and about 12 knots. I had a straight shot on a broad reach, 14 degrees behind Poplar Island to Bloody Point Light, then on to the Bay Bridge to Sandy Point Light without changing course. Most of the way was either a real broad reach or wing-and-wing. There was a constant haze, and the radio still kept saying storms. I traveled up the eastern shore side of the Bay and almost fell asleep several times. Tried to read, but the boat would yaw in the following rough seas and sailing took most of my concentration. Mid-morning I was passing Bloody Point Light. Prior to noon, I could hear the horn of Thomas Point Light on the other side of the Bay, and by noon, I had my first glimpse of the Bay Bridge, but then it would fade away in the haze. It was 1:30 pm exactly when I sailed true on course 14 degrees right through the center span of the bridge and about 20 minutes later I was passing Sandy Point Light. It started raining at the bridge.

Coming into the Magothy, I called my wife Sherry on the marine radio/telephone. She was at school, not more than five miles from me now, close to Mago Vista.

While going under the Bay Bridge, I noted hundreds of cars heading toward the ocean side. It was Friday afternoon, and, even though the weather was threatening now, they were calling for a nice weekend. I thought how those people would be at their destinations on the ocean front in about three hours. It has taken me three weeks to get back from there.

Soon I would be home. I came into the Magothy and photographed the "Old Man" marking the entrance at Gibson Island — the place that I had departed from on May 19th — today it is June 12th. It seems ages since I left that place on a rainy, mucky day, very much like the weather I am returning in. I wondered if it had ever cleared here and if I had just gone around in a big circle, in and out of bad weather.

I was sailing nicely when some fellows in a Bristol 27, from Bodkin Creek, tried to

Bay Bridge finally in sight.

Sailing under the Bay Bridge.

outrun me. I saw them trim their sails and duck down low to cut wind resistance. This was my cup of tea now and I trimmed also. The *Sherry D* dug her bow down and showed her stuff. We had one last fling and joy of working as a team. These guys really had a hard time keeping up and, in fact, they never did catch us until I slacked off to take another photo of them trying to catch us. As they came up to me, they expressed their compliments on how nice the *Sherry D* looked and handled. I thanked them and returned the compliment, telling them that this little boat was just now taking me home after a 465-mile trip around the Delmarva. They couldn't get over how old the boat was and what she had been through. They asked if I would like a beer to celebrate my return to the Magothy. I accepted and they sailed up close while I let my sails out and they handed a Michelob over to me. They then said their good-byes, went about and headed out the Magothy and back to Bodkin Creek.

I turned the bend at the Grachur Club, put the motor in the well, lowered the sails and turned on my Palauan tape. My son Sinclair (who is also a sailor), his wife Yvette, and my little grandson Nathan stood on the dock to welcome me home. It was 4:15 pm on the 12th of June, 1987.

Home.

Journey's End

Epilogue

I was glad to be home. A hot bath, a comfortable home with a nice family, a good meal and a warm bed with clean sheets is hard to pass up. I felt now that "I HAD" done it all. I accomplished what I had intended to do. I sailed completely around the shores of Delaware, Maryland and Virginia, the Delmarva Peninsula. For the most part, I followed the de Gast route and as far as I know, Robert de Gast and I are the only ones who have done this, behind the barrier islands and in a sailboat. For that matter, I know of no one else who has even attempted to do so.

In the final analysis, the success of the voyage was due to a desire and then the determination to just do it, (the mountain was there, climb it), a little patience, and a lot of luck. In the 26 days it took me to sail more than the 465-mile circle, I spent 19 days in mostly bad weather. I was never more than five or six miles from land at any one time, other than sometimes across the marshes behind the barrier islands, and most of the time on both sides of me land was in sight. It was an easy course to follow and anyone with basic sailing skills could do it, provided they had the right boat. It did take some concentration to play the tides, the winds and the currents. There were times when I didn't think that I or my boat would make it, but the confidence I had in my boat was the main consideration to go ahead. There was a time to take chances and a time to take cover. A time to be miserable and a time to feel good. To be logical was important. To be knowledgeable sometimes helped. To be humble, always helped.

Prior to starting this trip on the *Sherry D*, I traveled half-way around the world to swim with millions of jellyfish in a crocodile-infested lake in search of our geologic past. "I had done it all." I have sailed my little boat in circumnavigation of the Delmarva Peninsula. "I have done it all." Have I really done it all? What I really have done is only a fraction of what there is to do. I sit back and reminisce. I think now of the places I did not explore, and the waters I did not test. I think about the upper reaches of the Chesapeake; the Chester, the Sassafras and the Bohemia Rivers, not to mention the little creeks in between; then the Delaware Bay with all the wildlife refuges, the Murderkill and the Broadkill rivers and then Cape May on the other side of Delaware Bay. I didn't see enough of the Rehoboth Bay and the Indian River. Then the barrier islands; Assateague and the National Seashore where I never landed. Oh, how Assawoman Island beckons me back. Though I sailed behind them, I never set foot on Parramore, Hog and Cobb Islands. I missed the town of Cape Charles and the hundreds of little creeks that reach into the lower eastern shore of Virginia. I must go back to

Pocomoke, paddle a canoe from Snow Hill, find where I went wrong at Bloodsworth Island. See the Annemessey, the Manokin, the Wicomico and Nanticoke. I never did see the Honga River nor Hoopers Island Light, or even the Little Choptank. It would be nice to see the hundreds of miles of shoreline along the Choptank River and Eastern Bay. To sail the Miles River and come out to the Chesapeake again via Kent Narrows and the Chester River. Then too, there is the Western Shore, with its seven major rivers, and 6,000 miles of shoreline of the Chesapeake Bay alone to follow.

    I sit back in my soft chair in my nice cozy home and look out over the beautiful Magothy River. My little sailboat, the *Sherry D*, rests in her berth with sailcover still on. A wave slips in, she rocks and wiggles a little. We look at each other . . .

About the Author

Better known as "Bud," Howard Walker Schindler was born in Baltimore in 1925 and raised on the Magothy River in Anne Arundel County, Maryland.

Bud started sailing at age seven, after converting an old rowboat to sail. By age 10 he was racing his own Moth sailboat at regattas around the Chesapeake (his father would transport the Moth by tying it on the roof of his old Franklin auto).

World War II interrupted his life on the water, and after finishing high school, he was drafted at the age of 18. Bud adapted quickly to Army life and advanced through the enlisted ranks before being selected for OCS, where he earned his commission in the infantry. There were many interesting assignments in the US, Japan, Germany, Vietnam and Ethiopia. His love of the water was not forgotten. After being involved in several amphibious operations, he transferred to Marine Transportation where he was able to pursue an interest in oceanography.

He retired as a Lieutenant Colonel and returned, with his wife Sherry and their three children, to his original home on the Magothy River. In a desire to know more about oceanography, he went back to school and obtained an AA degree from Anne Arundel Community College. Studying water quality, taking and analyzing water samples, he volunteered his services in an effort to help in the restoration of the Chesapeake Bay and its tributaries.

SUGGESTED READING

deGast, Robert. *Western Wind Eastern Shore.* A sailing cruise around the Eastern Shore of Maryland, Delaware and Virginia. Johns Hopkins University Press, Baltimore, Maryland. 1975.

deGast, Robert. *The Oystermen of the Chesapeake.* Camden, MD: International Marine Publishing Co. 1970.

deGast, Robert. *The Lighthouses of the Chesapeake.* Johns Hopkins University Press, Baltimore, Maryland. 1973.

Barth, John. *The Sot-Weed Factor.* A fictional prose narrative of early Maryland. The Universal Library Edition, by arrangement with Doubleday & Company, Inc., Garden City, NY. 1964.

Stone, Wm. T., and Blanchard, Fessenden S. *A Cruising Guide to the Chesapeake.* Dodd, Mead & Company. 1983.

Lewis, Jack. *The Chesapeake Bay Scene.* A series of paintings along the Chesapeake shores where Lewis strives for the inner meaning of the scene — its human values. Jack Lewis, Bridgeville, Maryland. 1954.

Burgess, Robert H. *Louis J. Feuchter, Chesapeake Bay Artist.* The Mariners Museum, Newport News, Virginia. 1976.

Kensey, Charles C. *The Pocomoke River.* A booklet of personal memoirs on and descriptions of the Pocomoke River. Pocomoke City, Maryland. 1954.

Michener, James A. *The Watermen.* Selections made by Mr. Michener from his novel, *Chesapeake.* Random, Inc., New York, New York. 1979.

Klingel, Gilbert C. *The Bay.* A naturalist discovers a universe of life above and below the Chesapeake. Dodd, Meade & Company, New York, New York. 1951.

Lawson, Glenn. *The Last Watermen.* A true story of a Chesapeake waterman struggling to keep a way of life his family had passed on for eleven generations. Crisfield Publishing Company, Crisfield, Maryland. 1988.

Meanley, Brooke. *Birds & Marshes of the Chesapeake Bay Country.* Tidewater Publishers, Centreville, Maryland. 1983.

Warner, Wm. W. *Beautiful Swimmers.* Little Brown & Company (Canada) Limited, 1976.

White, Christopher P. *Chesapeake Bay, A Field Guide. Nature of the Estuary.* Tidewater Publishers, Centreville, Maryland. 1989.

Index

A
Adams Island, 116
Assateague Island, 61
Assawoman Island, 66

B
Bald cypress, 102
Barth, John, 28, 113
Bay Bird, 101
Bay Hundred Restaurant, 127
Betterton, 33
Beverly Plantation, 94-99
Bloodsworth Island, 113, 119
Bloody Point Light, 129
Blue Angels, 18
Bowers Beach, 44, 47
Bridge Walk, 20
Brown, Temple, 102

C
C&D Canal, 33, 36
Cairn, Captain, 113
Calvert Cliffs, 126
Cape Charles, 85
Cape Charles Channel, 86
Cedar Hall, 91
Cedar Island, 71, 72, 75
Cedar Island Bay, 75
Cedar Point Lighthouse, 123
Chance, 110
Chesapeake Bay Bridge, 20, 129
Chesapeake City, 33, 36
Chester River, 24
Chincoteague, 60, 61, 62, 63
Chincoteague Bay, 60
Coast Guard, Crisfield, 115
Cooke, Ebenezer, 113
Crisfield, 103, 104

D
de Gast, Robert, 5, 8, 11, 88
Deale Island, 110
Delmarva, 11
Delaware Bay, 37
Domes Island Nuclear Power Plant, 38, 42
Dykes, Jim, 69, 90-94, 112

E-F
Earthwatch, 12
Eastern Shoreman Restaurant, 69, 92

F
Ferry Point Yacht Basin, 12
Fleming's Landing Swing Bridge, 41
Franklin City, 111

G
Gibson Island, 20, 129
Gratitude, 25
Great Ocean Race, 11
Great Machipongo Channel, 78
Greenbackville, 60

H
Harborton, 88
Holland Strait, 109
Holland Island, 120
Holland, Paul, Capt., 113
Holland, Arby, 108
Hoopers Island, 113

I-J-K
Indian River Inlet, 50, 53
Jensen, Peter, 44
Kearns, Patricia, 123
Kegotank Bay, 65
Kiptopeake, 86
Knapps Narrows, 125, 127, 128

L
Lewes, 44, 50
Lewes Rehoboth Canal, 48
Limbo Straits, 113

M-N
Magothy Bay, 85
Magothy River, 18, 19, 129
Mill Creek, 123, 125
Murderkill River, 45
Nassawadox Creek, 86
Northeast Island, 116

O
Ocean City, 57, 59
Ocean City Inlet, 57
Okahanikan, 113
Okahanikan Cove, 114
Onancock, 89
Oxford, 127
Oyster, 82, 85

P
Palau, 8, 12
Patuxent River, 124
Pocomoke River, 90, 100
Poplar Island, 129
Pungoteague Creek, 87, 90

Q-R
Rehoboth Bay, 49, 54
Rock Hall, 25
Roosevelt Inlet, 48

S
Sabre World Cup Regatta, 127
Sandy Point Light, 129
Sassafras River, 33
Seven Foot Knoll Lighthouse, 24
Sharkfin Shoal, 109
Shettle, William, 94
Skipjacks
 Clarence Crockett, 113
 Caleb W. Jones, 107
Smith Island, 104
Smyrna River, 38, 42
Snow Hill, 93
Solomons Island, 124
Somers Cove, 103
Sot-weed Factor, 28, 113
South Marsh Island, 120
Steinhise, Thomas, 24
Still Pond, 33
Swan Creek, 25

T
Tangier Island, 104
Thomas Point Light, 129
Tolchester, 27
Tolchester Channel, 25

U-Z
US Navy's Blue Angels, 18
Virginia Inside Passage, 64
Wachapreague, 76
Wallops Island, 64
Webster, Dewey, 108
Wenona, 105, 108, 109
Wilkerson, Van, 69, 92, 104, 105, 107, 108
Williams Point, 93